6.95

Edge of Dawn

D0107906

Edge of Dawn

Esther Loewen Vogt

HERALD PRESS
Scottdale, Pennsylvania
Waterloo, Ontario

Library of Congress Cataloging-in-Publication Data
Vogt, Esther Loewen.
    Edge of dawn / Esther Loewen Vogt.
        p.   cm.
    ISBN 0-8361-3520-2
    I. Title
PS3572.03E34   1990
813'.54—dc20   90-33404
                                                                                  CIP

EDGE OF DAWN
Copyright © 1990 by Herald Press, Scottdale, Pa. 15683
        Published simultaneously in Canada by Herald Press,
        Waterloo, Ont. N2L 6H7. All rights reserved.
Library of Congress Catalog Card Number: 90-33404
International Standard Book Number: 0-8361-3520-2
Printed in the United States of America
Cover art by Susan K. Hunsberger
Book design by Merrill R. Miller
96 95 94 93 92 91 90 10 9 8 7 6 5 4 3 2 1

To my daughter
Shirley
precious, wise, thoughtful
and always loving

They that wait upon the Lord shall renew their strength;
they shall mount up with wings as eagles;
they shall run, and not be weary;
and they shall walk, and not faint
(Isaiah 40:31).

Dr. James McCauley, of the Kansas Geological Society, provided the facts regarding the lead and zinc mines which pockmark eastern Kansas.

All names and places in this story are fictitious, and any resemblance to persons, living or dead, is purely coincidental.

1

I watched the horizon deepen with pink as the sun crept above the brooding green hills far to the east. My little two-door Honda purred smoothly down the Kansas highway and I stepped on the accelerator to pass a slow-moving camper in front of me. The road was jammed with tourists, eager to escape the steel and concrete jungle of the cities, pulling their intrepid campers behind them.

On either side the view from the road was magnificent: wheat fields, knee-deep in furled grain, were now turning to gold, ready for harvest. I vaguely remembered spending one summer on my uncle Joseph Sutton's farm during wheat harvest with the sharp, hot smell of chaff forever in my nostrils.

Suddenly the scenery changed. The low roll of hills seemed to arch their backs like sinewy cats waiting for their food, reminding me it was time to stop for breakfast. I had been on the road since early morning, after nearly three days of driving from the West Coast. It would take another three or four hours before I reached Waylan in the southeast part of Kansas.

Waylan . . . where Meriweather Hall sat sedately on its outskirts, like a prim English lady in court.

I mulled over Paul Ward's cryptic message in my mind once more: *Your Aunt Corinda needs you, Amy. Can you come?*

I sighed, wondering for the thousandth time why my great-aunt Corrie hadn't summoned me herself if she needed me. I hadn't seen her in twelve years. That summer I was eleven and stayed at Meriweather Hall with her and Uncle Bentley while my parents were in Europe. She and I had corresponded spasmodically through the years since. Always an independent woman, she had valued her own self-reliance, never seeming to need anyone after Great-grandpa Daniel Meriweather had died. I remembered him as a fragile gray man with gentle brown eyes, always full of stories about his mines.

I recalled earlier childhood visits to Meriweather Hall with my mother. The big old brick house set in an old-fashioned garden surrounded by a low stone fence had always intrigued me. The place was unforgettable, and I would always think of my great-aunt as a permanent fixture in its shadowy walls. She surprised us when, at age fifty-two, she married Bentley Ward, a widower with three teenagers. After her marriage I had visited her only that one summer. Somehow I had never gone back, for the place was no longer the same after my mother died. Three lively young strangers filled the old mansion with their own laughter. My father had encouraged me to cut the ties. Why, I don't know. He had died just two years ago and now I was alone, and on my own.

Roadside signs ahead beckoned me to stop for gas and food. I slowed down and pulled up beside the nearest café. The hot tomatoey aroma of ketchup and hamburgers drifting from the open door drew me inside, and I slid into a booth near the window.

"May I help you?" a blond slim-hipped, tight-skirted waitress scurried beside me and slammed a glass of tinkling ice water on the table and flipped open her pad.

I glanced up at the regular menu offerings posted on the wall. "A plate of scrambled eggs, whole wheat toast, and a glass of chilled orange juice will be fine."

Sipping a bit of ice water, I bowed my head for a brief silent prayer and looked around the crowded room. The usual bustle of workaday people were grabbing a bite before hurrying to their jobs. Tourists were dragging in for a breakfast before heading down the road again.

"Pardon me, miss, may I sit here?" A fortyish woman, plump shoulders bulging from the narrow straps of a grimy striped blouse, eased her bulky figure into the seat across from me. Her hair was a dirty, ashy gray and hung in straggly wisps on either side of her round face. Her smile was shy, I noticed, and her blue-eyed gaze candid.

I smiled. "Of course. The place is crowded this morning."

"You a local? Or traveling?"

"I'm on my way to Waylan. I should make it in another three or four hours."

She paused and gave her order to the waitress, then eyed me critically. I knew my sky-blue pantsuit and blue knit blouse were fresh and clean, and my short brown hair combed and shining. I'd hastily tied a perky ribbon around my head to keep my hair from blowing into my face during the drive.

She grinned appreciatively. "My, you look nice. You married?"

I wasn't eager to carry on a personal conversation with a total stranger, but she looked pleasant, despite her disheveled appearance.

"No." I shook my head. "I'm a fifth-grade teacher, glad

11

to escape my classroom for the summer."

The waitress brought my order and I began to eat. The woman across from me studied her short, squat fingernails. Then she smiled wryly.

"Kids sure is hard to handle these days, don't you think? When mine was young. . . ."

Nodding now and then, I only half-listened as she recited her tale of woe. I had more important things on my mind than to hear about Alicia and her acne.

As soon as I finished my meal I nodded to the woman, hurried to the cashier's desk, paid my bill, and went out to my car. The warming June breeze fanned through the large elm, and I turned on the car's air conditioner as I drove away. Seeing the broad tree triggered memories of the old swing that had dangled from the elm in Aunt Corrie's backyard.

My mind wandered to my last summer there, when I had first met my three stepcousins. Eighteen-year-old Paul had swung me faithfully every night after dinner. I could still see his dark, serious face, his thatch of unruly brown hair, and wondered if he had changed much. I'd had a crush on Paul for months afterward. Once he'd pecked my cheek with a brotherly kiss, and I'd cherished it secretly for a long time.

Kathryn, a lanky sixteen, had worn her thick chestnut-colored hair tied back into a ponytail, but in a way that always looked correct and neat. Precise. That described Kathryn best.

Boyish, tawny-haired Colin at thirteen had been the clown, the cutup. Would twelve years have changed them? They had been kind, all three of them. And I thought again, why had Paul urged me to come?

12

Aunt Corrie had seemed so proud of them and they treated her with respect. Where were they now? I supposed Paul lived nearby, or else he wouldn't have written to me.

After my mother passed away, Dad and I had left Indiana and moved to the West Coast. My visits to Meriweather Hall had ended abruptly. I heard from Aunt Corrie faithfully at Christmas. Although her notes were always brief, she invited me to visit her any time. But since my mother's death my father never mentioned it. I never learned why. Meanwhile, Bentley Ward had died and Aunt Corrie's stepchildren had grown up. She lived alone in the big house, except for Annie Jane, who kept her company. The elderly woman had looked after the house and cooked for the Meriweathers as long as I could remember.

I grew up, too, went to college, and had just completed my second year of teaching fifth grade at Peter Conrad Public School. I was still Miss Amy Sutton, teacher. My summer plans included a leisurely cruise on the Caribbean in July, to decide whether or not to marry Eric Stone. Eric had taken a small country church and had begged me to become his wife. Somehow I needed time to think, to make sure I loved him enough to marry him. Everything seemed too pat right now, too easy. I needed to be sure.

When Paul Ward's message came I decided to spend a few weeks with my great-aunt before leaving on the cruise. It would be good to get back to Meriweather Hall. Perhaps I could recapture some of my delightful childhood days. If Aunt Corrie needed me, I was available. For now, at least. Maybe that's why I had accepted Paul's summons without question.

The next several hours slid past quickly, and signs announcing Waylan grew more frequent. As I drove into the city from the west, I looked at my map. I would have to drive through to the east part of town to reach the old house. Once it had been located along a well-traveled road, but I was certain the town had crept out and stretched to boundaries beyond. I was right. Well-kept ranch houses skirted the road, surrounded by wide treeless lawns and neatly trimmed shrubs. Once the old brick house had stood remote and distant from the rest of the town; now the recently constructed houses marched boldly up to the borders of the estate.

Through the trees ahead on the north side of the road I could make out the slate-gray roofs, the red chimneys, and my pulse pounded with nostalgia. I could hardly wait to embrace my great-aunt and revel in the dim coolness of the old brick house.

Slowing, I pulled up to the stone gateposts guarding either side of the short tree-lined drive that led toward the house. The estate had always seemed secluded behind a low mortared, ivy-covered wall, with polyantha roses and tamarisk crawling at its feet. Tall spruce and broad elms shaded the grass, angular maple shapes marched beside the drive, and formal flower beds and gardens stretched beyond the lawns to the rear.

Easing my Honda up the lane, I was stunned to see that the place looked unkept, the lawns patchy, and the graveled drive weed choked. The trees, always neatly pruned, now sagged under heavy foliage. Even the roses drooped on broken trellises. The place reminded me of the woman who had eaten breakfast at my table only a few hours ago.

Why had Aunt Corinda let the place go to ruin this way? She had always been proud of Meriweather Hall and once it had been a showplace in the community. A full-time gardener had kept it neat and tidy.

Pulling to a stop in front of the house, I drew my breath sharply. Now that I had arrived, a sudden apprehensive feeling overwhelmed me. As if—I shook my head firmly. No, it was just the shock of seeing the old place neglected and uncared for. Lord, why did you bring me back? I prayed silently.

Slowly I got out of the car and walked up the steps leading to the front porch. The paint on white colonnades was peeling. I noticed the scarred bricked edging around the steps, the sagging shutters, the worn varnish on the door. With a sigh I punched the doorbell and waited. The muffled sound of footsteps echoed through the hall and then the door opened with a rasp of hinges.

"Yes?"

Annie Jane stood there, more gaunt and gray than I remembered her, a shirred blue apron tied firmly around her thin waist. Her gray print dress was neat and clean and my gaze traveled to her face. I noticed the tired blue eyes behind bifocals.

"Hi!" I said with what I hoped was a cheery voice. "Remember me? I'm Amy Sutton. Tell Aunt Corrie I've come to spend a part of the summer with her. Where is she?"

Annie Jane's faded blue eyes widened, then she slumped forward a little. "You ain't heard? She—she's in bed and can't come down to see you."

2

I pushed my way into the wide musty hall and faced the elderly housekeeper. "I want to know why Aunt Corrie's in bed. Is she ill?" I asked, a chill numbing me at her words.

The older woman lowered her gaze and looked away. "She . . . it's because of the accident."

"What accident?" I almost shouted, my voice strident.

"Your aunt fell down the stairs and hurt herself."

I wet my lips and fought to control my emotions before I replied. "When was this?"

Annie Jane shrugged. "Oh, maybe three-four weeks ago."

"Why isn't she in the hospital?" I demanded.

"They's not much anyone can do," Annie Jane said, turning back to the door. "She laid in the hospital for three weeks, but about a week or two ago Paul brung her home."

"Is she hurt badly?"

Again Annie Jane shrugged. "She busted a rib or two, hittin' the landing."

I drew a deep breath and ran my fingers through my hair. No wonder she needs me, I thought.

"I think you should know they's a live-in nurse to look after her," Annie Jane went on. "Costs less that way."

"I want to see her," I said, pushing my way past her toward the stairs.

She barred my way. "Won't do you no good. Your aunt won't know you anyway."

"But I thought you said—her ribs—," I began urgently.

"She's not woken up yet." She stood in front of me like an army general, blocking my way. Then suddenly she relented. "But I guess you might as well, seein' as you've come all the way from Californy."

I followed Annie Jane up the gray carpeted stairs. For a moment I faltered at the landing where it turned right. Then bracing my shoulders I reached the top of the steps and headed for the upper hall. I remembered Aunt Corrie's door was the first to the left of the hall that had seemed to stretch on endlessly when I was a child.

In front of the door I grabbed Annie Jane's arm. "Did you say she has a live-in nurse?"

"Name's Crosby. She's got a cot set up so's she can check her all the time. There ain't much you can do." Her voice carried a slight edge, I thought.

Before we could enter, the knob turned and a large woman in her late fifties blocked the entrance. She wore a prim old-fashioned white linen uniform with three or four hospital pins studding her broad chest. Her kinky hair was a mousy-gray, obviously permed to the hilt, a nurse's cap perched on the curly top. Her eyes were veiled behind dark-rimmed glasses and her rough, contoured face bore a dour look. One eyebrow twitched as she tried to push me aside.

"You can just stay away," she said brusquely in a ragged voice. "Nobody's going in."

"But I'm her grandniece and I've come all the way from California," I blurted, feeling both a little angry and ridiculous. "You can't keep me out."

Stepping aside, she opened the door with a resigned gesture as though helpless at my "intrusion."

I moved across the threshold and started to cross the large softly carpeted room. Aunt Corrie's white iron bed had been pushed almost to the southwest corner, to make room for a gleaming enameled table holding the usual sick-room supplies.

The white-sheeted mound on the bed didn't move as I came and stood beside her. The thin, fragile face with closed eyes lying on the pillow and framed in short silver hair, seemed bloodless. I gulped. The once-animated face of my great-aunt bore no resemblance to this manikin on the bed.

Reaching out, I touched one white cheek. "Aunt Corrie," I whispered, "it's me, Amy. Paul said . . . you needed me, so I came."

The figure lay motionless on the bed. I stood for fully five minutes stroking the ashen cheek, but there was no response. Shock waves raced up and down my spine, for I certainly wasn't prepared for this.

At a sound behind me, I dropped my hand and turned. Mrs. Crosby motioned me away.

"You been here long enough. You'd better go," she said in a low, guttural voice.

I hurried from the room, almost dragging her with me, and turned to her in a blaze of anger.

"I demand to know what's been going on, Mrs. Crosby!"

The heavy shoulders shrugged brusquely. "How should I know? I wasn't here when it happened."

"No, but as a nurse—"

"If you want to know you'll have to ask Mr. Paul, when he comes from work."

She whirled back into Aunt Corrie's room and slammed the door. Feeling like an intruder, I turned and walked slowly down the stairs. So Paul lived here at Meriweather Hall, too. I could hardly wait until he came home so I could pepper him with questions.

Annie Jane hovered in the kitchen doorway down the hall, fingering the hem of her apron absently.

"Had lunch, Miss Amy?"

"Lunch?" I echoed, suddenly remembering my last meal ages ago in the little greasy café along the highway.

"No, Annie Jane. If you'd fix a sandwich, please. . . ."

"I'm warming up a kettle of soup. Lunch will be fixed in half an hour." She disappeared back into the kitchen.

Troubled, I went out to my car and brought in my luggage. Maybe if I hurried, I could unpack before I ate. Carrying my two bags up the stairs left me only a little winded. I remembered my old room across the hall from Aunt Corrie's and tried the knob. The door swung open easily. I set down my bags and went first of all to the tall east windows. Drawing back the heavy green drapes, I pushed open the sashes on both.

The room was almost as I remembered it, with its dark mahogany furniture and thick gray rug. The walls, papered in a muted green design, seemed to emphasize the forest green of the drapery, and the two oil paintings on the west and south walls picked up the green in angry seascapes.

I set the first bag on the brown-tufted bedspread and began to unpack. Hanging up my white suit and an array of colorful blouses and skirts in the large walk-in closet, I thought I heard a sound in the doorway. Was Mrs. Crosby going to protest my moving in so near my aunt's room?

Without turning, I said over my shoulder, "This was always my room when I used to come to visit, and I. . . ." Pausing, I turned my eyes to the doorway. A child of perhaps eight years stood watching me. Her long red-blond hair hung to her shoulders, revealing delightful spatters of freckles over the bridge of her nose and trailing off into plump cheeks. But her most striking feature was her eyes—like a pair of green agates chiseled in granite. There seemed neither life nor light in them.

"Hi!" I called out gaily. "I'm Amy, and this will be my room. Who're you? I don't think we've ever met—"

"I'm Brandy," she cut in. "Daddy and me live here. Grandma Corrie looks after me," she spoke in short, clipped sentences.

"But isn't it just the other way?" I countered. "You have to look after her, don't you?"

She shook her head fiercely and the granite eyes sparked green fire.

"No! No! You'd better leave. We don't want you. Don't you hear?"

With a twirl of her sturdy figure she was gone.

3

Who was this child? And what was she doing here? She had talked about "Daddy." If she was Paul's daughter, she had none of his dark good looks. And where was the mother?

What disturbed me most was her strangeness. I sensed something uncanny about this child. Her eyes had reminded me of green agates, like cat's-eye marbles, and equally as lifeless.

There was one way to find out. It was lunchtime, and I headed for the kitchen to ply Annie Jane with some questions.

The elderly housekeeper was bending over the stove stirring something aromatic in a small kettle as I came in.

"Lunch almost ready?" I asked by the way of greeting.

She turned slightly. "Your soup's simmering on the back burner. I'm fixin' Miz Corinda's broth, and don't want to be bothered about nothing else right now."

"Oh." I grimaced slightly. Her response wasn't exactly overwhelming.

Rummaging in the huge white cupboard, I found the stack of blue porcelain bowls I remembered as a child. Some were chipped from long use. The heady aroma of beef and string beans rushed to my nostrils as I dipped out the thick, creamy vegetable soup.

21

"Annie Jane," I began, "I didn't know . . . about Brandy. She—we met while I was unpacking."

The gaunt little woman didn't answer. I could hear the soft clink of spoon against the kettle as she continued stirring the broth.

"Is she Paul's child?" I ventured again, setting my bowl on the large square white-painted table that seemed to dominate the huge old kitchen. She turned her head and looked directly at me.

"They moved in here last winter," she said, her voice brusque. "Miz Corinda felt Brandy needed a woman to manage her. But I guess the child got almost too much for her at times."

"Why? Where is her mother?"

"Ask Paul. Maybe he got answers. I don't." With a sudden movement she spooned the broth into a thick mug and bustled out of the kitchen.

I ate my soup slowly. I had really stumbled onto a nest of questions. For answers I had to wait until Paul came home from work. Meanwhile, where had Brandy gone?

Finishing my meal, I washed the bowl and spoon at the old-fashioned porcelain sink, dried them, and put them away. Annie Jane apparently wasn't too eager to return to the kitchen while I was there. She probably resented my coming, too.

Opening the back door, I stepped onto the long open porch that faced north. It was partly shaded by a bedraggled clematis vine that clung to a broken lattice. The blossoms drooped in the warm sun and I noticed the blue petals dappling the ground. The cobblestone path that led among the trees toward the kitchen garden was overgrown with weeds. Wide elms shaded the backyard, and bluegrass

22

grew tall and uncut in their mottled shade.

Walking down the path, I paused, delighted at the pair of ropes that dangled from the high branches of the elm on the left. The old swing was still there. I could almost hear my squeals of laughter when I as a child clung tightly to the ropes while a solemn-faced Paul Ward pushed me back and forth, a ritual we had practiced each evening before twilight. How I'd adored those moments!

I walked silently toward the swing and fingered the ropes gently. They were a bit frayed from wind and weather. Twelve years was a long time. Would Paul have changed much? Would he have the same serious features, and did the same intense emotions play over his dark face? Obviously he was married and had fathered a child. I wondered about Kathryn and Colin. Where were they? Did they ever visit their stepmother? I felt a stab when I thought how little I knew about them. We had simply lost touch through the years, and I felt a trifle sad. Why hadn't I insisted on coming back for a visit now and then?

For the next hour or two I roamed over the grounds to the rear. The little gray henhouse was deserted, and the old horse barn beyond it sagged like a tired old man. Colin had once dared me to climb the hayloft to look for eggs, brown and warm from some domestic-minded hen. I soon learned to scramble up the ladder and find the eggs, and he pretended to be upset because I found the eggs first.

As I started toward the barn I thought I heard a car in the drive, so I hurried back to the house. A rather nondescript blue sedan made straight for the carriage house that served as a double garage. I paused beside the broken trellis entwined with a few straggling pink roses, half afraid to meet whoever had arrived. I wasn't sure I was ready for the answers I might learn about Aunt Corrie and her strange illness.

The car door slammed, and I saw a tall, intense young man come toward me. I recognized Paul immediately. The shock of dark hair tumbled over the parting in the middle, and the same solemn frown creased his brow. He wore a uniform of blue slacks and a short-sleeved shirt, open at the throat. His eyes seemed troubled, his jaw muscles working. When he saw me, he took big strides toward me and reached for my hand.

"So you came, Amy," he said in the same deep voice that echoed in my memory. "I'm glad you're here. It's been so long." He dropped my hand and turned away.

"Yes, Paul, I'm here. But there's so much I don't understand. I—"

"Let's go into the house," he cut in abruptly, taking my elbow and guiding me casually up the front porch to the door.

Flinging his arm away, I whirled on him. "Paul Ward, what's going on anyway? Why wasn't I told about my great-aunt earlier?"

His grin was a trifle lopsided. "I guess I was pretty vague in my letter."

"Vague!" I yelled. "I could count the words on ten fingers!"

Leaning against the doorjamb he idly traced the red bricks of the side of the house with his forefinger.

"Good thing I was here," he said, his voice low. "Ever since Sue became—ill. . . ." He drew a sharp breath. "After my wife got sick, Corrie-Mom asked us to move in with her. She and Annie Jane were alone, and Brandy needed looking after, so I agreed. It was a good deal for us both.

24

Corrie-Mom wouldn't be alone, and Brandy had someone to look after her."

"Where is Sue?" I asked.

"She . . . she has a debilitating illness—an aggravated case of rheumatoid arthritis—and has been at the Connors Sanitorium for the past four months. It's affected Brandy, and she has spells of being unruly and hard to manage. Sometimes she's almost incorrigible."

He paused, as though the truth were painful, and shifted his position. I saw the deep agony mirrored in his eyes.

"I'm sorry," I said quietly. "I'm sure it must've been hard on you all. But what really happened to my great-aunt? Annie Jane said you'd tell me."

Shrugging, he let his gaze wander to the rim of maples that bordered the drive. The late afternoon wind stirred the leaves and they hissed softly.

"There's not much to say. About a month ago she—she fell down the stairs. She struck her head and cracked some ribs. It's a miracle she wasn't killed."

"And her paralysis?"

He shook his head. "The doctor says there's nothing to be done."

"Is it permanent?"

"She hasn't given any indication that she can speak, although she can eat if she is fed. Her legs—her body. . . . It's hard to see her lying like—like a statue. It would take a miracle. . . ."

His voice faltered, and he opened the door and motioned me into the house.

I took a deep breath and laid a hand on his shoulder. "Paul, why wasn't I notified sooner? After all, I'm her only living blood relative."

"Amy!" He jerked away from me almost angrily. "You haven't been in touch with your aunt in years! You haven't cared a hoot, have you? We felt no need to call you." His words were bitter.

"Then why did you write me now?"

He gave his head a slight shake. "There are times when Corrie-Mom seems agitated. We decided maybe she needed someone around, a person she knew. Besides, somebody needs to take charge."

"You said 'we.' Do you mean—"

"Kathryn and Colin agreed this would be a good idea."

"Then they're around?"

"Colin has his own apartment, and Kathryn lives in a town house. She—she and her husband, Grant Lawrence, are separated."

I turned away. So Aunt Corrie's stepchildren still lived in the area. My thoughts returned to the fragile white figure upstairs in the dim bedroom.

"What are Aunt Corrie's chances of coming out of this condition?" I went on. "Surely some do recover!"

Paul looked grim and a spasm crossed his face. "We have small hope that she will, Amy. As I said before, it would take a miracle. And I don't believe in miracles!"

4

At dinner that night I sensed the tense atmosphere even in the small dining room. The oval table covered with a white damask cloth was set with one of Aunt Corrie's sets of better china. It was my favorite, the creamy white porcelain with a scatter of tiny pink roses on each piece. The crystal and silver shone in the gleam of the small chandelier that hung from the ceiling. I remembered the room so well. Here all the informal family meals were served. The larger, formal dining room was opened only for "company."

Paul sat across the table from me, with Brandy between us at one end, a sly gleam in her hard green eyes. I wondered what went on in that strange eight-year-old head.

"Annie Jean's cooking gets better all the time," I said, trying to make conversation as I attacked my roast beef with a serrated knife. "I guess she will always feel she belongs in the kitchen."

"Well, she's paid staff," Paul said, buttering a whole wheat roll.

I smiled a little at his remark. I realized she had probably never been paid much, for Aunt Corrie had always considered her more of a companion than a servant. So I wondered why the gaunt, elderly woman insisted on maintaining her "hired help" status. Of course, Annie Jane was a "fixture" here and that is how she apparently wanted it.

"How about Mrs. Crosby? Surely she eats somewhere," I said after I finished my baked potato.

Brandy's eyes changed to a shifty glitter. "She gets a tray. We wouldn't want her here anyway."

"But why? She could join—"

"No, she couldn't. She's gotta watch Grandma Corrie. At least that's what Aunt Kathryn says. Certain people we don't want around." She glared at me.

Paul looked at me and shrugged his shoulders, letting me know it wasn't his idea.

Suddenly Brandy reached for her glass of milk. I saw her flip it over, the milk sloshing on the cloth and running in swift white rivers toward my plate and onto my lap.

Jumping up, I grabbed my napkin and tried to sop up the wetness from my apricot-colored slacks.

"Brandy! What did you do that for?" Paul demanded, glaring at his daughter.

My gaze was icy as I looked at him. "I saw her tip the glass deliberately, Paul."

"I'm sorry, Amy." He got up and headed for the kitchen. I followed him, found a towel, and wiped the milk from my slacks as best I could. Paul attempted to clean up the mess on the table. I heard him scolding Brandy while he moved plates and silverware out of the way.

When I returned to the table Brandy sat with her head bowed, a frown narrowing between her eyebrows, trying to look contrite. Yet I had the feeling it was an act.

"Sorry, Amy," she said with a pout. "I was . . . clumsy."

I patted her shoulder and smiled. "It's okay, Brandy. I'm washable and so are my clothes."

"Aren't you gonna turn me into a frog?" she asked, her stony gaze fixed on me.

"I said it's okay, Brandy."

Sitting down, I ate the rest of my salad and peas. Neither Paul nor Brandy spoke, and I sighed a little. So many strange things were happening for which I had no answers. I was glad to finish my meal and go up to my room.

I changed into a blue-flowered duster and flopped into the chintz-covered easy chair near the open window. Already the twilight had faded and stars winked one by one in the mauve heaven.

Paul's earlier words still grated sharply in my ears. *I don't believe in miracles,* and my mind went back again to twelve years ago. Aunt Corrie used to take me to Sunday school in the magnificent white-steepled church on the hill.

"Remember God loves you, Amy," she had told me often. I had imagined God placing his arms around me and giving me a loving squeeze, and the feeling comforted me. My heart warmed at the memory of the Sunday morning I lagged behind and asked my teacher, Mrs. Henner, how to let Jesus into my heart. She simply explained God's love for a lost world and how he had sent Jesus to be the sacrifice for our sins. I had offered an artless prayer, asking him to be my Savior and Friend. Through the years I had walked with the Lord, and he had never let me down. I had known him as a God who could do miracles, and in my faith and trust I believed he would act, if one believed. I would always be grateful to my great-aunt for leading the way to a living faith for me.

But none of Aunt Corrie's stepchildren ever went to church the summer I was there. Small wonder Paul had no idea what faith and forgiveness was all about.

That I would spend a part of this summer here at Meriweather Hall, I knew. Yet what could I do to be of help? To do anything worthwhile? It seemed fruitless as I looked back on the hours since my arrival.

Bowing my head, I prayed for wisdom.

"Lord, you alone know why I'm here, because I'm not sure why I came. Please help me."

Paul had suggested someone should "manage things." Besides, Brandy needed me, I decided. The child was full of hurt and anger which she was taking out on everyone around her. Perhaps I could provide love and understanding, even try to heal some of her frustrations, her hurts.

Another thought hit me. I knew Aunt Corrie had faithfully read her Bible in years past. Yet now her trancelike state made it impossible. What if I read the Scriptures to her daily? Perhaps God's Word might seep into her troubled mind and in her subconscious state comfort her. I'd heard of stranger things happening.

The moon slid from behind a cloud rack and scattered silver light over the neglected gardens. I felt the urge to walk outdoors and let the peaceful night steal over me.

Slipping into a pair of white slacks and yellow knit top, I took a light sweater from my closet and made my way quietly down the stairs and stole out of the house.

Shadows bent through the rim of maples along the drive and mottled the white moonlight on the unkempt lawns with dark patches.

Pulling my sweater close around me, I sauntered down the graveled drive. The evening was silent, with only a faint chirp of crickets from the barns and an occasional twitter from a birdling in its nest. I reached the end of the drive and paused beside the broken gatepost.

The old peacefulness of Meriweather Hall stole over me and I sighed contentedly. Perhaps the Lord knew what he was doing when he led me back here. Maybe I needed some of the tranquillity I'd always known here.

Hearing the sound of muffled footsteps behind me, I turned. Paul, his dark face white in the moonlight, came toward me.

"I heard you go out, Amy," he said softly. "You okay? After Brandy's cheap trick at the dinner table—"

"I'm fine, Paul. I just came out to see if the old magic was still here!"

"Is it?"

I flung out my arms wide, as if to embrace the grounds. "Oh, it's changed terribly. But the memories. . . ."

"I know. They'll always be here."

We started back toward the venerable brick house, our shoes scuffing lightly on the gravel.

"I'm really glad you came," he said awkwardly, "and I'm sure you are still wondering why I sent for you."

"Things are beginning to fall into place, Paul," I said with a short laugh. "When I discovered my great-aunt in that dazed state I couldn't imagine why you needed me here at all. But now I think I know."

We had reached the porch and he stopped abruptly under the porch light. I thought I saw a shadow flicker over his face.

"Why do you think you're here?" he asked, his voice a trifle gruff.

"For one thing, maybe I can help Brandy. Now that Aunt Corrie can't, perhaps it's up to me."

"I appreciate the gesture, but don't count on changing things quickly."

"I'll try, anyway." I eased myself onto the stone railing and leaned against a colonnade. "How long do you need me here?"

"How long can you stay?"

I laced my fingers together. "A month. Six weeks. I've signed up to go on a cruise in late July."

"Fair enough. Don't tie yourself down, Amy."

"Another thing I can do is read to Aunt Corrie from the Bible," I went on. "I don't know if it will help but at least I would feel I'm doing something for her spirit, just as she did for me years ago."

Paul nodded. "Bless her, she tried with us too, but I guess we were beyond reach by the time she married Dad." His voice still held the bitter edge.

I wanted to cry out: It's never too late for God. But I knew this wasn't the right time.

"Perhaps I can help Annie Jane, like shopping for groceries, and giving her a hand with the cleaning. She's not as spry as she used to be!"

"If she'll let you!" he burst out. "She's quite opinionated. But it'll be good to have someone take over a few responsibilities here. So much has fallen on me. With my job at the plant I don't have any time to spare."

I got to my feet, stretched, and started for the door. "I understand. Maybe Mrs. Crosby will let me help take care of Aunt Corrie too, so she can get a break now and then."

"Don't count on anything here, Amy. Mrs. Crosby's a stubborn old horse. She takes her job seriously and allows no interference."

With a quick good-night I went back into the house and walked upstairs to my room. Paul was the same as ever, I thought—somewhat negative, and very serious. I'd handle Mrs. Crosby my own way, I decided.

Sleep overtook me quickly when I crawled into bed. Perhaps because I was tired, or maybe I'd discovered my purpose and could pursue it with eagerness and determination—and resignation.

With a stab I remembered Eric Stone. He would have to wait for his answer. I wasn't ready to think about my future, for too much of the present demanded my attention now.

After breakfast the next morning I took my Bible and headed for Aunt Corrie's room. The door was closed as usual, and I knocked lightly.

"Well, who is it?" Mrs. Crosby's gruff voice called out.

"It's me, Amy. May I come in?"

She opened the door a crack and peered at me. Her glasses had slid down on her nose and she reminded me of a workhorse wearing blinders.

"What do you want?"

"I'd like to see my aunt. One of the reasons I came here—"

"I'm not done with her bath."

"Can't I help? I mean, I'd like to relieve you of your duties once in awhile," I said in my most cheery voice, hoping I sounded warm. "Give you more time for yourself."

"Don't need you, so stop interfering." The door slammed in my face.

Shaking my head, I walked back into my room. So much for offering to help the crabby nurse, and handling her, I thought.

It was a perfect June morning that clamored to be savored in the backyard. As I came through the kitchen, Annie Jane was finishing up the breakfast dishes. I laid a hand on her shoulder and took the dish towel from her.

"Here, let me help you. You're swamped with more work than necessary. If I take over some of the work—"

"I'll manage," she said curtly, jerking the tea towel away from me, her eyes smoldering.

With a shake of my head I went out the back door. Would all my efforts to help be rebuffed? Perhaps Paul was right. Change wouldn't come easy at Meriweather Hall.

To my delight I saw Brandy on the swing under the elms. She wore a blue sundress and her red hair was blowing straight behind her like a bright canvas sail. Pattering down the walk, I ran toward her and gave the swing a push. It swung out and up, then back. As I pushed, it moved back and forth. Brandy squealed with delight.

"This is fun, Amy!" she cried. "Make me go higher."

"Better hang on," I shouted. "We don't want you to fall."

For several minutes I swung her, until I stopped and leaned against the rough bark of the elm with a breathless laugh.

"Let me . . . rest a bit," I panted, allowing the swing to go slower.

When it stopped, Brandy jumped off and flew toward me. "That was a lotsa fun. Can we do it again sometime?" Her green eyes seemed to light up, and I was pleased to see the gleam in them.

"Sure. We'll do it often. I remember the summer I was eleven and came here to visit, and your daddy used to swing me like this. I thought it was fun, too. But that was a long time ago."

She wiggled her bare toes in the grass and looked down. I could almost see the green agate eyes turn to stone.

"That was before I had a . . . a Momma. . . ." Her voice trailed off.

Cautiously I reached out my hand, but she ignored it. At least, for a little while Brandy had responded to me. I remembered Paul's words last night:

"Don't count on Brandy's accepting you."

"Sure," I said aloud, trying to sound cheery. "We'll do it again sometime."

Without a word she turned and fled into the house. I followed her slowly up the stairs. When I reached the top step she was waiting for me. Her green eyes narrowed and she glanced at me slyly.

"How would you like it if someone pushed *you* down the stairs, like they pushed Grandma Corrie?"

I froze at her words. What did Brandy mean? Had—*had Aunt Corrie been pushed?*

5

Pushed? The thought stabbed me. What did Brandy know? Or was it just a whim of overactive imagination?

I was caught in a dilemma, for I couldn't confront Brandy with more questions. Since the child was moody and at times almost incorrigible, as Paul had suggested, I must proceed with caution. Perhaps the best thing now was to forget her rash outburst and concentrate on helping Aunt Corrie.

Back in my room I picked up my Bible and headed across the hall. This time I would demand some time with my great-aunt.

Mrs. Crosby eyed me shrewdly when she opened the door to my urgent knock.

"Well?"

I patted the Bible in my hand. "My aunt used to take me to Sunday school when I was a child," I said. "She probably misses church. So I thought if I read to her from the Scriptures it might soothe her. I know she may not even be aware of what I'm doing, but I want to try. What do you think?" I looked at her coarse, flabby face and saw the tense facial muscles relax.

"Well, I guess it won't hurt her none," she conceded slowly. "But it won't help neither," she added brusquely.

"All I ask is a chance to try."

With a reluctant sigh she moved aside and let me into the sickroom. I had to admit that Mrs. Crosby, for all her brusqueness, was taking excellent care of her patient. Aunt Corrie's gown was fresh and the linens on the bed spotless. The room was orderly and neat.

As I moved beside the bed I turned to the nurse. "Since I'll be right here, feel free to run an errand. There's no need to wear yourself out, hovering over your patient every minute, especially now."

"It's what I'm paid to do. Besides—"

"Please take a walk. Get out for some air."

"Well. . .," she hesitated. "I'll step out for a whiff of fresh air, but only for a couple of minutes."

"Do that. If I need you, I'll call. I promise."

She left the room heavily and I turned to the quiet figure on the bed. If only I could get through to her somehow.

I touched the white forehead gently and placed my palm against one frail cheek. "It's me, Aunt Corrie. Amy Sutton. I'm here to—to do whatever I can for you."

Pausing, I watched for the slightest flicker of interest. The features were as gaunt and still as ever.

"You know, maybe you can hear me and maybe you can't," I went on. "But I'm going to pretend you hear every word I say. I'll always be grateful to you for taking me to church and Sunday school on my visits here years ago. It was in your little church that Jesus Christ became real to me. This same Jesus is as real and powerful today as he was then, Aunt Corrie. Don't you agree?"

I paused again to wait for a response. There was none. Opening my Bible I flipped to the fortieth chapter of Isaiah and began to read verse 31:

" 'They that wait upon the Lord shall renew their

strength; they shall mount up with wings as eagles; they shall run, and not be weary; and they shall walk, and not faint.' Aunt Corrie, trust that verse!"

Her features were motionless and showed no sign that she heard a word I said. Still, if dropping God's promises into her subconscious could soothe her spirit, it would be my chief mission in Meriweather Hall these next few weeks.

As I heard muffled footsteps along the hall I looked up. The manner in which Mrs. Crosby marched into the room was like a commanding army general, and I knew my visit with Aunt Corrie was over.

I got to my feet and arched my neck to relax my tired muscles. "Thanks for letting me visit my aunt," I said. "I hope you enjoyed the walk."

She motioned me toward the hall. "Someone's waiting to see you, Miss Sutton."

"Me?" I hurried across the room and stopped in the doorway. I immediately recognized the laughing, carefree figure with the tousled blond hair standing beside the door.

"Colin!"

He grabbed me with a quick bear hug. "So Amy has returned. I wondered if you'd ever come back to me," he said lightly, stooping to plant a warm kiss on my cheek. "Let's go down to the library where we can talk."

Arm in arm we strolled down the stairs together. Colin hadn't changed, and underneath he seemed like the same charming, fun-loving thirteen-year-old I remembered through the years.

The dim old library was cool and pleasant with its mahogany shelves of musty books, the dusty mantel, and faded Brussels carpet that covered the floor. Colin steered me to the rust-and-green floral sofa. He sat down on the brown velvet chair opposite.

"Let me look at you, Amy," he said, searching my face intently. "Still brash and impudent, I'm sure. So now we'll catch up on the news. It's been a long time, Amy. Too long."

I leaned back, folded my hands on my lap, and looked at him. His face was ruddy and his smile spontaneous. I could never forget his laughing gray eyes and the provocative cleft in his chin. The casual tan slacks and brown-and-green knit shirt he wore looked expensive. That matched with Paul's report that Colin worked in the bank.

"So how's the banker?" I prodded lightly. "Paul mentioned your job."

He leaned back, stared at the ceiling, and rolled his eyes. "Your interest—and I mean that literally—overwhelms me. Yes, I work in the bank, although I haven't gotten much past being a teller."

"You will. Anyhow, it's a start toward better things. I was surprised to learn that Paul and Brandy have moved here to Meriweather Hall. Do you have your own place?"

He crossed his legs before answering. "Right. That is to say, I rent a fabulous apartment at an atrocious price."

"And you haven't married?"

"Oh, you know I've been waiting on you." The twinkle in his gray eyes gave him away, and I laughed.

"Is this a proposal? I should've been warned I'd get another one."

He uncrossed his legs and leaned forward. "Another proposal? Don't tell me male swains are falling all over you already."

"Already! You know I'm an old maid of twenty-three, so it's not that bad," I said with a short laugh. "But right now there's Eric."

"Eric." He took my hands in his. "And you can't decide between him and me? I'll make it easy, Amy. I can tell you right now that I'll waste no time helping you make the right decision."

"Oh, come now, Colin," I said, snatching away my hands. "You know I could never compete with your charm. If I'd constantly fight off beautiful girls—"

"Well, about this guy Eric. He isn't some rich big shot who keeps you dangling in your schoolroom, is he?" he cut in.

"No." I shook my head. "You won't believe this, but Eric pastors a small country church."

"Whew!" Colin's whistle jolted my eardrums. "You? A preacher's wife? I can't believe it. Amy Sutton, you were always full of life and mischief."

"Maybe I still am. Eric is lots of fun and he's a terrific guy. But I'm not sure he's right for me. Maybe not seeing him for awhile will show me what is right."

"I'll do all I can to persuade you that you're making a mistake to say yes to him. Know that?"

"Thank you. You're sweet, Colin. But to me marriage is a sacred thing. I won't enter into it lightly." I paused to twist my birthstone ring. "I definitely want God to guide my decision."

Colin got up and walked to the tall west window. He stared out at the unkempt landscape and spoke without turning.

"So you still hang onto that Sunday school faith you brought home from church the last summer you were here."

"Do you remember that, Colin?"

He whirled around. "Do I! Corrie-Mom held you up as a pious example for months after you left. Oh, not that she pestered us, but if Amy could become goody-goody so could we. Still, somehow she never got us started to church. Not even after Dad died."

"Why not?"

He came and stood in front of me, his hands behind his back. "Paul and Kathryn had become rebellious teenagers by then and I went along with them. So I honestly don't know why we refused. We figured she made a will to leave you all her worldly goods instead of us, so why do anything to please her?" He shrugged his broad shoulders awkwardly.

"But Aunt Corrie wouldn't do that!" I cried. "I mean— she wouldn't change her will just because I was the one who took the step of faith. She's not like that at all. Besides, why should you go to church to please anyone? The Lord—"

"Thing is, we don't know what her will reads," he cut in, avoiding my question. "That's something she's never told us."

"If you really loved her, her money wouldn't matter."

Colin sat down on the brown chair again. "Of course, I love her. But some puzzling things have happened lately. It seems that her income has dwindled. That's why she's let the gardener go and neglected other repairs on Meriweather Hall."

I knew that Bentley Ward was almost penniless when he had married Great-aunt Corinda, and I think that must've been what had kept my father from allowing further contact with her. Dad always felt that Uncle Bentley had married her for her money. I could never accept that, because I saw how gently he treated her. So whether or not she left everything to her stepchildren or to me, it had never really bothered me. I was back here because she needed me, whether she realized it or not.

The silence between Colin and me grew awkward. I decided that whatever hurt was between my great-aunt and her stepchildren shouldn't dampen my friendship with them.

"Colin," I said quietly, "let's forget the hurts of the past and concentrate on the present."

He grinned boyishly. "Sure, Amy. I'm sorry for having gotten carried away."

"What about Kathryn? Where is she now?"

"My sister's a newspaper woman, top-notch reporter for the *Waylan Star*, and she's off at some convention right now."

"Her marriage—is it going to survive?"

"I don't know. She and Grant are separated. That's all I know. She doesn't share much with us."

"She was always so correct and precise," I said. "Aunt Corrie used to say Kathryn was a real lady. She always knew what she wanted."

"Yeah. She used to pretend she was a princess and Meriweather Hall was her castle. Sometimes she played Cinderella, too."

"And Aunt Corrie was the wicked stepmother?"

"Right. Poor Corrie-Mom. I don't think she ever really knew how Kathryn felt. I was embarrassed for my sister sometimes. But lately she's changed."

"In what way?"

"She does all she can. Picks up and pays her medicines,

runs errands for Crosby—stuff like that. She can't seem to do enough for Corrie-Mom."

"I'm glad to hear that. And how do you feel about my great-aunt?"

"Now?" Colin tapped his finger on the knees of his tan slacks. "I love her. We all do. And I feel sorry to see her laid up like this, Amy. I wish to God it hadn't happened!"

"And the past?"

"Sure, I'll admit we gave her some bad times, but that's all over. She's special to us now."

I couldn't help remembering Brandy's words this morning, and I took a deep breath, not sure it was best to mention it.

"Colin, let me ask you something. Do you think Aunt Corrie might have been pushed down the stairs?" I plunged in without prelude.

Colin's gaze narrowed and his lips became two thin lines around his even teeth. "What a horrible thing to say, Amy!" he exploded.

I shook my head. "I'm not saying I think it happened, but from what Brandy told me—"

"Don't believe everything that poor, mixed-up kid tells you. She's got a wild imagination and then some."

"Yes." I got up from the sofa and started toward the door. "I've already learned that."

"On the other hand"—Colin was behind me, his words almost whimsical—"there's always a chance she could've been pushed. But who in the world would do a crazy thing like that?"

I stepped into the hall and steadied myself against the carved oak banister. Yes, I thought. Who'd do a thing like that?

6

I left the library, Colin's words ringing in my ears. Who in the world would do a thing like that? Unless—unless someone wanted her dead. But who? Colin insisted the three of them loved their stepmother. And if that were so, who else would want her out of the way? Perhaps he was right. Brandy could be imagining it.

The next afternoon I persuaded Mrs. Crosby to let me read to Aunt Corrie again. The big, brawny nurse showed little resistance this time. She left the door open to the hallway as she marched out.

I had just flipped the pages of my Bible to the passage in Isaiah when my eyes caught Brandy's freckled face peering around the edge of the door.

I motioned to her. "Want to come in? We'll visit Aunt Corrie together."

She came in slowly, her reddish hair a bit askew from play and her green eyes almost soft. Pausing beside the bed, she reached out and touched Aunt Corrie's arm.

"She looks so—so still. I wish she'd say something."

"What would you like her to tell you?" I prodded gently, almost holding my breath.

"Like she used to. She told me about Jacob and—and Rachel. And she also told me that someone loves me."

"And who's that someone?" I asked softly.

"God. She said God loves everybody. But if he does, why did he let Momma get sick? Didn't he love her? And why did Grandma Corrie go bumpety-bump down the stairs?" Her words were almost angry. As if she questioned that a God who loved her would let this happen.

"Brandy." I spoke gently. "Brandy, things happen to everyone, good things and bad things. God wants us to be big and strong and brave, like it says in the Bible: 'They that wait upon the Lord shall renew their strength . . . shall not be weary . . . shall walk, and not faint.' We need to trust. . . ." I paused.

The softness in Brandy's green eyes hardened to a stony agate, and the cat's-eye gleam was back.

"But why can't Momma walk? Why is she in that hospital bed, not at home with Daddy and me? Why did God let it happen?"

I shook my head. How could I answer this child? Her hurt was growing so deep.

Closing my Bible, I reached for her hand, but she flung me off.

"I don't need you!" she burst out bitterly. "Why? Amy, why?" Then she turned and fled from the room.

My gaze followed her, and I ached for her. Touching Aunt Corrie's forehead, I leaned over and said quietly. "We have so much to do, so many hurts to heal. Don't you see? You've got to get well. Brandy needs you. We all need you."

I drew back after my outburst. Why had I poured out my frustration on my great-aunt like this? She couldn't hear a word I said.

To my amazement a sudden flicker of interest crossed her face, then it became as impassive as ever. As if, for a second—but of course, she *couldn't* have heard my words.

At that minute I heard Mrs. Crosby's heavy footfall. I picked up my Bible and hurried across the hall to my room.

The overpowering fragrance of my favorite blend of perfume, *Moon Song,* rushed out to meet me. As I walked toward the dressing table, I saw on the striped bench a yellow puddle that ran in rivulets down the side, and the shattered bits of glass on the floor. My first thought was that Annie Jane had wielded her dusting brush too vigorously. But I had never known her to be clumsy. Then it hit me: Brandy. She was in one of her black moods and had probably smashed the perfume bottle deliberately in childish anger.

The spurt of rage that swept over me was soon overpowered by pity for the child. Incorrigible? Yes, maybe. But Brandy also had her tender moments. It was up to me to try to bring out those gentler times. I decided not to mention the incident to her.

Scooping up the shards of broken glass and mopping up the spilled perfume with a Kleenex, I tossed the mess into the wicker basket that stood beside my bed.

I spent most of the morning in my room, puttering with duties I'd neglected for the past several days, such as doing my nails and brushing my hair back into its natural sheen.

As I came down the stairs for lunch, Brandy was nowhere around. But of course the child had haunts I knew nothing about.

Annie Jane was stoically uncommunicative as usual, and I ate my whole-wheat and cheese sandwich and sliced tomato in silence.

The afternoon dragged. I browsed restlessly in the library, looking for something to read. Oh, yes, there was the dog-eared copy of *Gulliver's Travels* I'd devoured as a child, and the well-thumbed copy of *Black Beauty*. I remembered the afternoon I'd been engrossed in the story of the beautiful horse when Colin had found me.

"Hey, you've been cooped up long enough. Why not ride a real black beauty instead of just reading about it?" he'd chided.

I had laid the book aside as I followed him out to the barn, always ready for a challenge. The groom had saddled the black and the roan and soon we rode through the gate on the dim trail that led toward the mines to the east.

I had almost forgotten about the abandoned lead and zinc mines that pockmarked the land stretching nearly a mile east of Meriweather Hall. At one time very productive, the mines had been largely responsible for my great-grandfather Meriweather's wealth. He had invested his money wisely and apparently his income and that of Aunt Corrie's stemmed from these investments.

We used to play in the rocky, hilly area around the mines but were forbidden to go near the entrance of the nearest one, which he called Old Number Two. I wondered if it had been blocked off securely. Some day I would go and see.

Now I glanced at my watch. Four o'clock. Time to check with Annie Jane to see if she needed vegetables from the kitchen garden. A teeming crop of lettuce and endive was producing some good foodstuffs for the table. I had offered to pick all the elderly housekeeper could use and she seemed relieved not to have to bend over to gather what she needed for the table.

Donning my wide-brimmed sun hat, I picked up the basket from the butler's pantry and set out for the garden at the rear of the house. The path that led to the fenced-in plot was well worn and I breathed deeply of the warm June air. A vegetable garden was one thing Aunt Corrie always insisted on; it was therapy for her to hoe and weed, and pick the first ripe beans and tomatoes of the summer's crop. She had always counted on plenty of fresh vegetables in the family menu.

Bright marigolds flanked the fences and wild fennel grew in profession along the edges. Bees buzzed over the flowers, and here and there a butterfly winnowed over the pungent gold petals. A heavy, warm somnolence lay over the peaceful afternoon. Annie Jane had been unable to keep ahead of the weeds that were beginning to choke the neat rows of lettuce, beans, and carrots beyond the tomato patch. More than likely Aunt Corrie had planted this garden in the spring, before her accident.

With a pair of garden shears I soon cut an enormous amount of leaf lettuce and pulled up a few young onions and radishes.

Hearing a step behind me, I spun around. Paul stood at the end of the lettuce row, still dressed in his blue work uniform. He waited until I reached him, then took the basket from my hands.

"Thanks," I said, with a wave of my shears. "I see Aunt Corrie's garden still grows—and so do the weeds."

"And so does everything else around here—the shrubs and trees that badly need pruning." A thin smile touched his face as he fell into step beside me and we walked to the rear of the house.

Before we reached the kitchen door he stopped and laid a hand on my arm.

"Look, Amy," he said, a trace of concern on his face, "I appreciate what you're trying to do for Brandy, like inviting her to visit Corrie-Mom with you. But—"

"She told you that?"

"Yes. She came running to meet me the minute I got home."

"Was she pleased?" I asked, somewhat surprised at her action.

"Well—she just said you and she had visited Grandma Corrie and that she didn't know if she liked it or not."

"Did she also tell you that she smashed my favorite bottle of perfume?" I said lightly.

He glanced at me anxiously. "Of course not. But I'll deal with her. I'll buy you—"

"Please don't. She was angry and she took it out on what she figured was very special to me. It's not that important."

"I know you're trying to help Brandy, but please don't expect too much. She finds it hard to understand about her mother, and she sees in you someone who has stepped into her mother's place in this household."

"I know that, Paul. Still, I want to help her, if I can. Remember—with God all things are possible."

"You really believe that, don't you?" His voice was bitter.

"Yes, Paul, I do. I'm even praying for Aunt Corrie to hear the Scriptures I read aloud to her."

"You surely don't expect her to recover, do you?" he asked somewhat incredulously.

I smiled a little. "All I know is that with God all things are possible."

"Well, if there is a God, he'll have to be a big one to accomplish that!" I leaned against the porch trellis, took off my sun hat, and fanned my face. Looking into Paul's troubled eyes, I felt sudden pity for this man. I had always admired him, for he was conscientious and full of deep concern. But he lacked the most important thing in life—faith in God.

"You're a skeptic, aren't you, Paul?" I asked bluntly.

He looked away with an embarrassed glance. "I only know it's useless to pray. If there is a God, he doesn't bother with the likes of Paul Ward."

"But God is great enough, Paul," I said almost vehemently. "If he chooses to restore Aunt Corrie, it's possible." I paused for a minute and the silence hung heavily between us. Then I plunged on. "Paul—do you—do you think anyone would want her dead?"

The dark look of anger was back in his eyes. "Colin told me what you said yesterday. All you have to go on is one of Brandy's wild tales!" He stalked up the porch and slammed into the kitchen.

I moved away from the trellis and let out my breath slowly. Why should Paul have been so angry with the idea? It didn't make sense to me.

7

Paul seemed to avoid me for the next several days, but I was busy with so many activities that I didn't have time to miss our casual chats. Without asking Annie Jane, I took the vacuum sweeper upstairs and cleaned the hall and large, spacious rooms and dusted the furniture. Brandy followed me around silently like a stray pup, her green eyes stony. She seldom responded to my efforts at conversation but seemed to consider me as someone she must watch—although why, I couldn't determine.

I also spent about ten or fifteen minutes each morning at Aunt Corrie's bedside. Usually I read our verse about "wait upon the Lord." The rest of the time I simply talked to her. I told her about my schoolwork as though she heard every word, although she never gave any indication that she did.

"Let me tell you about Jason Dobbs," I told her one morning. "Jason's a scamp but sharp as a tack. One Friday I asked the class to write a theme on 'Why I am an American.' I almost exploded with his response. He said that the *Untied States* Declaration' gave him freedom to go fishing during school hours if he wanted to, but the principal did not, and he wasn't sure if he should obey his country or his school. I guess the *Untied States* lost that round!" I chuckled aloud, then heard a giggle behind me. Brandy stood in the doorway, her green eyes soft and gentle as a kitten's.

51

"That Jason's a dummy," she volunteered as she slipped into the room and came close to the bed. She stared at Aunt Corrie's quiet figure, then grimaced. "I thought maybe she'd smile just once."

"She's still sleepy," I said. "Maybe she didn't hear."

"Then why do you talk to her?"

"We don't know how much she does hear. Maybe she hears more than we think, so I *pretend* she's listening." I paused, then took Brandy's hand. "Would you like to tell her something? Just maybe she's listening now."

Brandy stretched on tiptoe, and leaned over the silent form on the bed. I saw the child's face muscles working, as though trying to find courage to say something. Finally the words spilled out. "Grandma Corrie, I—I love you. I—I didn't mean to . . . knock over that—that fancy vase with the ivy that was in the front hall. It—I guess I was just . . . mad." A tear stole down the freckled cheeks.

My own eyes blurred. I sensed deep down Brandy was not incorrigible. She was obstinate at times, perhaps. Yet she had suffered a great deal of hurt in her young life. No wonder she lashed out at whomever or whatever she felt was responsible.

She drew away, and her gaze held mine for a minute. There was a genuine sorrow in the green depths. Laying a hand on her shoulder, I whispered,

"I wouldn't be surprised if she heard. You've told her you're sorry. Now please put the matter out of your mind."

Our discussion was interrupted by a footstep in the doorway. I looked up to see a slender, beautiful woman framed there. Her warm brown hair fell in waves and ringlets to her shoulders and her piquant face was lit up by a quiet smile.

"Kathryn!" I cried. "Is it really you?"

As she came into the room I noticed that her smart Caribbean blue suit fit her petite trim figure as though it was made just for her, and her peach-colored blouse softly outlined her firm young form. Her nose, always pert and abrupt, lifted slightly with a toss of her brown head.

"So you're back, Amy," she said in her bright, amusing way. "It's about time."

"It's been too long. I realize it now." I got up and we hugged each other briefly. Brandy stood by and watched us, her face pensive.

"So what have you been up to?" I went on after I moved back to my chair beside the bed.

"I just got back from the Penwomen's Convention in Boston," she said. "I had a fantastic time."

"I'm sure you did. After all, you must be a topnotch writer with the position as ace reporter for the *Waylan Star*."

At that moment Mrs. Crosby returned, which signaled that our visit with Aunt Corrie was over.

Brandy disappeared down the hall as we started from the room. The dour nurse touched Kathryn's arm.

"Don't forget to stop by the pharmacy and pick up Miz Ward's medication. She's almost out."

"I will. Don't worry," Kathryn said, and we went downstairs together and headed for the library. She kicked off her high-heeled black pumps and stretched out on the floral sofa. I sat down in the brown velvet chair opposite and crossed my legs.

"What's this all about?" I asked. "The medication, I mean."

"Oh, that's my job. I see to it that she gets her medicines. I also pay for them."

I raised an eyebrow as I uncrossed my legs. "Pay . . . for them? But why? What of her money? I thought she was loaded."

"She was." Kathryn drummed her fingers on the armrest.

"What happened?"

Kathryn shrugged her slim shoulders. "Ask Colin. He's the banker. He says her funds are dwindling and we'd better cut back on expenses."

That's what Paul had said. Of course, it explained the neglected state of Meriweather Hall. Since Aunt Corrie could no longer afford a gardener the place was falling into ruin.

"My great-grandfather was considered to be a wealthy man," I said. "His zinc and lead mines were quite productive at one time."

"Yes, but some petered out. He sold those that survived, remember?"

Yes, I remembered. But Aunt Corrie had invested the principal and her income had been more than adequate through the years from the interest alone, my father always maintained.

Kathryn pleated the tie of her expensive peach-colored blouse with her fingers. "How long do you plan to stay, Amy?"

"I'm not sure," I said. "Since my school was out I decided to find out what Paul meant when he wrote that Aunt Corrie needed me. Imagine the shock when I found her helpless."

"Yes, isn't that too bad? It's hit me too. I can't get over it because I still feel Meriweather Hall is my home, although I live in the condo Grant and I bought after our marriage.

I drew up my knees and hugged them with my arms.

"I'm sorry the two of you are having problems and have separated. Any chance of ironing them out?"

She shrugged her shoulders again. "That remains to be seen. I—I've tried. But we're both pretty obstinate, you know."

My thoughts raced to Eric. Could I ever be the kind of wife he deserved as minister of the gospel? I too had so much of my own stubborn will to master.

The phone rang just then and I got up to answer the extension in the library. It was Colin.

"Look, Amy, how about going out with me tonight? It's time you got out of jail and had some fun."

"I'd be delighted, Colin," I said eagerly.

Kathryn had slipped her pumps back on her feet and was standing in the doorway. "I gotta run, Amy. That my baby brother you're going out with?"

I laughed. "Oh, yes. He's still the same charming, witty Colin I always remembered. And good for a few laughs, which is what I need right now."

"And how," she added, her gaze narrowing a bit, "do you remember me?"

I came up to her and touched her shoulder. "Kathryn, you were always so precise, so perfect, so sure of yourself. I felt I could never reach your level. You're still that way, I think."

Her laughter trilled after her as she clicked down the hall and out the door. Yes, Kathryn always knew what she wanted out of life and she'd get it too. I admired her strength and determination. She was least vulnerable of them all.

When Colin called for me some time later, I had showered and changed into a beige two-piece knit dress with brown buttons and a narrow brown belt around my waist. My hair was brushed and shining, and I'd fashioned a pair of tiny gold earrings into the lobes of my ears.

Colin whistled as I came down the stairs, and I knew that the pains I had taken with my preparations for our date were not in vain.

"Wow! All gussied up, and beautiful besides," he said, taking my arm. "I'd forgotten how good lookin' you were underneath all that brash exterior. If your preacher could see you now, he'd throw daggers at me for conning you into a date."

"My preacher, as you call Eric, can't see me, so let's forget about him, shall we?" I countered.

As we started for the door Brandy bounded down the stairs and yelled shrilly, "Amy! Don't go away. I want you to stay with me!"

Paul was beside her in a moment and placed an arm about her shoulders. "Don't be silly, Brandy. Uncle Colin is just taking Amy out for dinner. She'll be back before you know it."

"Bye, Brandy," I called out with a wave of my hand. "I'll swing you on the old rope swing tomorrow after breakfast. See you then."

Colin steered me through the front door and down the steps toward his old white Porsche. He must be doing well at the bank to afford a heap like that, I thought,

As he opened the door on the right side for me, I managed a graceful bow.

"Cinderella is overwhelmed with her prince's elegant chariot," I said whimsically.

He got in beside me and grinned boyishly. "I hope this crate won't turn into a pumpkin at midnight. It's put me in hock deep enough so that it might decide to do just that. It's not new any more, you know, but it still cost plenty."

We laughed as we drove through the gateway and down the highway east of the city, then turned onto the blacktop leading toward the lake that gleamed like polished pewter. The winding road snaked back and forth along the hillside, with fashionable homes arranged in mounting levels. After a turn or two I could look down on the gray roofs of Meriweather Hall in the semidarkness. Finally Colin pulled up before *The Golden Lady,* Waylan's most exclusive restaurant.

A long, glassed-in veranda was set above the terrace, with white covered tables in a row, where diners could sit sheltered and still look out upon the terrace and see the view. The ceiling slanted steeply overhead, with skylights and hanging lamps.

I decided to forget about my great-aunt and her baffling "accident," Brandy's strange behavior, and all the puzzle-pieces that had bombarded me since my arrival in Kansas. Tonight I would enjoy myself with Colin. I needed his wit and carefree spirit.

"What shall we order?" he asked after he had seated me at one of the small white tables and the waiter had brought our menus. "How about hummingbird's wings broiled in Vienna sauce, with ambrosia to drink?" he said lightly.

"Anything at all," I said, "as long as it agrees with the contents of your pocketbook."

"Ohhh." A mild groan escaped him. "You don't know what you're saying, woman! If I'd take you up on that we'd dine on hamburgers and French fries!"

"As bad as that? And all because of the Porsche?"

"The Porsche and my expensive apartment and high living," he added lightly. "But the eternal smell of money in my nostrils all day is overpowering."

"Well, why take me to dine in style? I'd have been satisfied with a hamburger and a slice of tomato."

He reached out and covered my hand with his strong palm. "I figured your preacher wouldn't be able to afford *The Golden Lady*. He'd probably consider it too—worldly. And I wanted you to know what living's like, just once."

I withdrew my hand. "It's sweet of you, Colin, but you don't have to do this just to impress me, you know."

"Maybe not," he said quietly. "But I'll wager you're not dining too royally at Corrie-Mom's these days either."

"We manage. Besides, Eric's doing okay. He's certainly not destitute."

"Well, I hope for your sake he isn't!"

"Colin—," I began, wondering how much I should pry. "Colin, what do you know about Aunt Corrie's money situation? I understand her funds are dwindling. Kathryn says you probably know the state of her bank account."

"It's true. Her savings have been sharply withdrawn and her checking account is rather low. Her social security barely keeps her bank balance solvent."

"Who's in charge of her money, now that she's incompetent? Surely someone. . . ."

Colin looked away quickly, then he drew a deep breath. "She decided to appoint someone as her guardian after my father died, someone with the power of attorney, in case she ever became unable to manage things on her own. Al McDivitt has been in charge for some time now, even when she was able to write her own checks. And Al has dropped hints recently that her money's going fast."

"What will this mean for Aunt Corrie's future?" I asked pointedly. "And the future of Meriweather Hall?"

He shook his head. "I don't know, Amy."

"What about this Al McDivitt? Is he trustworthy?"

"Your great-aunt seemed to think so. He worked for the mining company for years, and his reputation in the community is apparently solid. We haven't ever questioned it."

The waiter brought our dinner of duck with mushroom sauce and tiny new potatoes with parsley, and our serious conversation ended.

Still, I couldn't help wondering about the state of Aunt Corrie's finances.

8

The days slipped by like pearls on a string, days bursting with warm June sunshine, or suddenly gray with a fleeting summer shower.

I often sauntered outdoors after Annie Jane's evening dinners to feel the wind dying on my face. Tonight I swung myself on the low stone fence and watched the sun dip below the horizon. The red glow at the rim of the world faded into pink, and the sky turned slowly from azure to the delicate blue-green of a robin's egg as twilight stole with a shadowy dimness over the landscape. There was only the quiet *zewzzewwzzewwzzew* of cicadas in the shrubbery to mar the stillness.

Here was Meriweather Hall at its best, its shabbiness subdued in shadow, its beauty alive in the quietness of dusk. I cradled my knees in my arms and breathed deeply of the evening air. Somehow all my troubles seemed to shrink when I felt God's peace steal over the world. God's arms seemed to be around me as though I were a child, assuring me that all would be well.

I clambered down rather stiffly from my perch and made my way in the semidarkness toward the old brick house. Its magic stole over me again as it had when I had visited it as a child, and I caught my breath sharply.

"Amy?"

I heard someone call my name softly, and hurried along the shadow-drenched path toward the house.

Paul was leaning against the colonnade of the porch, staring into space when I rounded the corner.

"Did you call?" I asked, pausing on the walk.

"Yes. I wondered if you were still out there. You watching the sunset?"

"Nothing equals a Kansas sunset, you know."

"Don't you miss California? Waylan must seem awfully dull after the glitter and bustle of Hollywood."

"Hollywood?" I laughed. "I guess I'll never quite get over the tinsel and excitement to some degree. Yet, I'll have to admit that nothing spells home like Meriweather Hall."

"Then you'd like to come back here to live—even if it wasn't yours, should Corrie-Mom die?" His tone was slightly cynical.

I drew a sharp breath and faced Paul squarely. "I'm not thinking about inheritances the way some people around here seem to do!" I retorted.

He moved from his post and stepped up to me, tilting my face toward him.

"Please get that chip off your shoulder, Amy. It doesn't become you," he said gruffly. "All I meant was, what if . . . what if she loses this place? What if. . . ."

I stepped back quickly and placed my hands on my hips. "What are you driving at, Paul Ward? That Meriweather Hall will pass out of Aunt Corrie's hands? That she stands to lose it?"

He shook his head, and in the deepening twilight the shadows lay dark upon the fine planes of his face.

"I'm only surmising. I hope it won't come to that. But we

must face what might be inevitable."

Without a word I swung around and ran up the steps and slammed through the front door. This was a possibility I refused to consider. There had to be another answer.

I was tired of their sly innuendos, their talk about wills and inheritances. As long as Aunt Corrie is alive, I promised myself, I'll see that she stays here! I'll do what is necessary to make sure she will.

Running lightly up the dim stairs, I went into my room. It was almost stifling in the evening air, and I turned on the fan. The old brick house had never been air-conditioned, but it was built sturdily, with attic fans and shutters and other features that had kept it pleasant even on hot, sweltering days.

Slipping out of my cool sleeveless dress I donned a thin blue nightgown. Then I got out my Bible and sat under the floor lamp to read. Somehow my thoughts turned to "patience." I wanted to taste success, to see immediate results. But that, I learned from the Bible, didn't always happen. Again the passage from Isaiah was impressed upon my mind, to "wait upon the Lord."

"Lord, show me what my job is," I prayed, "and let me do it faithfully, then leave the rest with you." I laid my Bible on the bedside table and crawled between the sheets.

Bright sunshine streamed through the east windows of my bedroom when I awoke the next morning. I hurried downstairs for breakfast, eager to begin my day. Somehow I felt it would be a glorious one, and I could scarcely wait to savor it.

As usual, I knocked on Aunt Corrie's door promptly at ten, then waited for Mrs. Crosby to leave the room. The large, stern nurse took her time that morning, pausing to

62

fold back the clean sheet from my great-aunt's face. She pulled the window shade against the brilliant sunshine that crept through the southwest windows.

"Have a good walk, Mrs. Crosby," I said somewhat impatiently, wanting to be alone with Aunt Corrie. "It's such a beautiful morning."

"Walking tires me," she grumped. "Besides, I've met every weed and thorn on the place. If I walk any more I'll wear out my shoes. Can't afford that."

I chuckled. "No, we can't have that. Why not sit on the back porch and watch the bees in the honeysuckle vines on the old grape arbor?"

"Humph! Who wants to get stung by a bee?" she muttered as she clomped out of the room. I heard her heavy footfalls disappear down the hall.

"Well, Aunt Corrie," I said, pulling a chair close to the bed, "it's just you and me again. God's given us a gorgeous day. What shall we do with it?"

She lay quiet and immovable, and I paged through my Bible until I came to our verse. I read it slowly and distinctly.

" 'They that wait upon the Lord shall renew their strength; they shall mount up with wings as eagles; they shall run, and not be weary; and they shall walk, and not faint.' It's like this, Aunt Corrie. . . ." I paused, suddenly aware that she had opened her eyes, and her sharp blue gaze was obviously on my face. I drew my breath sharply. Could she hear what I was reading and saying to her? Did this mean she *could* come out of her groggy state? That it wasn't a real coma? In my excitement I was eager to continue.

"Aunt Corrie . . . Aunt Corrie, you just looked at me!

You saw me, didn't you?" I babbled almost incoherently. "You—!" Suddenly the eyes grew dim again and there was no further recognition in them.

My eagerness was dampened a bit and I decided not to tell Mrs. Crosby. The crabby nurse would disbelieve me anyhow. Yet there was a bounce in my step as I hurried down the hall, after Mrs. Crosby had returned to resume her duties in the sickroom.

When I started down the stairs, I heard the front door slam and looked down to see Kathryn in the lower hall.

"Kathryn!" I called out excitedly. "Guess what?"

She looked up expectantly at me as I flew down the stairs and hugged her.

"What's up, Amy?" she asked, a puzzled look on her face.

"I was reading to Aunt Corrie just now, and suddenly— you won't believe this, Kathryn, but her eyes were open and her gaze followed me, *as though she understood what I was reading!* Isn't it great? Do you think she'll comprehend what we say to her now?"

Kathryn continued to stare at me, as though she found it hard to believe. Then her gaze narrowed. "That would be a miracle, wouldn't it?" she said finally.

"Well, don't you believe in miracles?"

"Do I believe in God? I'm not sure," Kathryn said slowly. "Sometimes I think I do. Next time I don't know. Tell me about God. Is he real to you?"

I took her arm and led her into the library, and we sat down across from each other. She looked neat and trim as usual, dressed in a dark blue-and-white striped dress with matching navy slippers. She leaned forward as though eager to hear me out.

"Is God real to me?" I repeated her last phrase. "Oh, yes! He is what makes life meaningful. Through Jesus Christ, God's Son, I have eternal life when I accepted his free grace which he provided by dying on the cross. There's . . . I can't really explain or describe it, but Christ is my strength, my anchor."

Kathryn listened silently as I continued to share my faith with her. If only Paul and Colin would listen. Now it was enough that Kathryn gave me attention.

A few minutes later she got to her feet and started for the door. "Excuse me, Amy. I'd better pick up her medication bottle," she said. "She needs a refill before the pharmacy closes. Thanks for your time, Amy. You're rather remarkable, did you know that?"

With those words she hurried from the library.

I sighed. Had Kathryn really been interested? Or was she, like Colin, too full of the world to be concerned for spiritual things? Still, I felt encouraged, both about Aunt Corrie's awakening and Kathryn's willingness to listen.

When Colin called about a date for that night I was eager to go. At six I took a warm, relaxing bath and slipped into a sheer red dress with a swirl of ruffles around the neckline and a narrow self-belt around my waist. I wore white high-heeled sandals and brushed my hair until it shone. I felt terrific, and I'm sure it showed. But I knew I could never match Kathryn's look of sophistication.

Colin called for me at seven. He was dressed in expensively cut casuals as usual.

"Hey, Amy, you look awfully sharp!" he exclaimed when I came down the stairs. "Like a flame of a candle that will be snuffed out, if I'm not careful. Tell me, do you buy all your clothes with me in mind? After you plan how you can best charm me?"

I pirouetted before him. "Of course. Only I think it's the other way 'round. You're charming me into a reckless mood, Colin Ward. When I'm with you I forget about the rest of the world!"

"That's what I want." He took my arm and we left the house and got into the car. This time we drove to a quiet little café at the west edge of town. It was decorated simply, but the food was good. Since the encouraging news about Aunt Corrie, I felt everything tasted great.

After we had finished our broiled steaks with creamed broccoli and a salad, I leaned back in my chair.

"You know, Colin, this is the perfect ending to a fantastic day," I said, smiling at him across the candle-lit table.

He reached over and touched my hand. "Tell me what's made your day so special. You seem to have a secret you're bursting to share. Have you decided to accept my marriage proposal?" he said lightly.

"Oh, come now, Colin. Why do you need a wife? How would you have time to squire around every pretty girl in town if you were married? And what would that do to your eligible bachelor image?"

"You've got a point there, Amy," he said slyly. "Besides, dates keep me constantly broke. But something's on your mind. I sensed it the minute I walked into the house. Let's have it."

"Colin—" I withdrew my hand and tucked a stray curl behind my ear. "Colin, you'll never guess what happened today. I was reading to Aunt Corrie from Isaiah again, and suddenly—suddenly she looked at me. I mean, *really looked at me.* As though she saw me! Colin, isn't that splendid news?"

He scratched the back of his head before replying.

"That's—that's great, I guess. But she didn't stay awake, did she? She slipped right back?"

"No, she didn't stay awake. But that doesn't mean—"

"Still, what if she never comes back altogether? Wouldn't it be a letdown? The doctor says there may be those fleeting moments when she may *seem* to wake up. Yet this can be only temporary."

"But Colin, don't you believe—"

"I just don't want you to get your hopes up, Amy."

I drew back, disappointed. I guess I'd hoped Colin would be ecstatic about it, the way I was. Well, I had to remember that neither Colin nor Kathryn had seen Corinda Ward in her fleeting moment of consciousness. No wonder they couldn't get excited about it.

The next morning when I came out of her room after our time together—she had seemed as far away as ever—I found Brandy waiting for me. Her green eyes held a glinty sparkle.

"Amy," she said, reaching shyly for my hand, "would you like to see Thomasina's kittens? They're up in the hayloft."

"You mean, the loft in the barn? That's another place I haven't visited in years," I said with a chuckle. "Wait until I change into jeans and an old shirt and leave my Bible in my room."

"Take your time," she called out over her shoulder. "I'll wait for you in the barn."

Quickly changing my clothes, I hurried out of the house through the back way and followed the weedy path that led toward the large, weather-beaten gray barn. The horses that once occupied the stalls had long gone. I recalled the horseback rides with Colin and Paul to the mines, Colin riding recklessly ahead. Paul, sober and subdued, was my dutiful guardian because Aunt Corrie always urged me to mind him. He probably hated it as much as I did.

The stale odor of hay and manure still clung to the empty stalls as I entered the barn's dim interior, but everything looked the same as I remembered it: the hay mangers, the oat boxes, and the musty harness that hung from the nails.

Brandy sat astride one of the stanchions, waiting for me.

"Where is Thomasina and her family?" I called out as I blinked to accustom my eyes to the semidarkness.

"Up the loft. You're not scared to climb the ladder, are you?" she said, scrambling from her perch and crawling nimbly up the wide rungs that led to an open shaft to the loft above.

"I was never afraid," I called as I climbed after her. "We used to crawl up here every night, Colin and I, to look for eggs. Some old biddies insisted on laying their eggs in the hay."

The wide-board floor of the loft was shiny from the many tons of hay that had been shoved from one end to the other through the years to feed the horses. Only a few wisps lay scattered along the walls now. Thick dust sifted through the cracks and sent gold-speckled spears of morning sunlight dancing onto the large bare room. The gabled window at one end let in enough light to take away the gloom.

Brandy scurried to one corner where I heard tiny mewing sounds. The gray-and-white striped mother cat watched cautiously as the little girl picked up one after another of the four kittens. Two were gray, one was yellow, and the fourth was a pure white.

"Oh!" I cried, scooting down beside Brandy. "They're adorable!"

"Which one do you like best?" Brandy asked, cuddling the yellow one and a gray one in her arms.

I pretended to ponder. "M-m-m. They're all absolutely perfect. Somehow, though, I think I prefer the white one."

"That's Snow White," she said. "This yellow one's Cheesey, and the two gray ones are Mousey and Minnie."

"Oh, so you've already named them. You chose the very best names," I said, reaching for Snow White. "Think she'll let me hold her?"

"She's slippery so you'd better hang onto her," Brandy warned. "Quick, too. Don't let her get away."

"Well, that makes two of us quick ones," I said with a short laugh, stroking the kitten's white fur. I was enjoying Brandy's comradely spirit. She finally seemed to regard me as someone she could trust. Perhaps she was beginning to accept me as a part of Meriweather Hall.

At that moment Snow White slid from my hands and jumped away. I scrambled to my feet and started after the kitten, rushing headlong toward the opening in the floor.

Just as I reached for Snow White, I felt a sudden push. Reeling against the blow, I lost my balance and plunged down the open shaft, landing on the hard dirt floor of the barn, my forehead grazing against one of the horse stalls. Pain seared my head, and as I touched my brow with my fingers I felt a wet stickiness. For a second I grew faint. Then my head cleared.

I heard Brandy's voice above me. "See?" she taunted. "That's what happened to Grandma Corrie, only worse. Poor Grandma Corrie. Maybe you'd better leave, Amy, before somebody gets you too!"

9

I picked myself up gingerly and slowly made my way out of the barn and to the house. The fact that Brandy had pushed me didn't bother me as much as her words. This was the second time she had hinted that Aunt Corrie had been pushed. If this were true, why would anyone want to harm the dear little lady? Who would do such a thing?

I groped my way up the narrow back stairs and went to the bathroom to wash my face. The cut on my forehead was slight and after the first stabbing pain it throbbed only a bit as I bathed it with cool water. Band-Aids were in the medicine cabinet. I covered the wound neatly and went to my room.

Throwing back the quilt on my bed, I stretched out full-length. Although I felt only a little shaken, I was sure the fall had bruised me. I'd probably be stiff and sore by morning.

I thought over my experiences. I should've known that Brandy considered me an intruder. She still wasn't ready to accept me. Somehow I couldn't get her words out of my mind.

Who had pushed Aunt Corrie? And why? The question nagged at me. Colin? He always seemed short of money, yet spent it lavishly. Working in the bank, he might have found some access to Aunt Corrie's funds.

Paul? He was so vehement when I had first mentioned Brandy's accusations. Paul's wife was in an institution and the exorbitant cost of keeping her there must be a heavy drain on his income. Both Paul and Colin would have reasons for wanting Aunt Corrie dead—if it meant an inheritance at her death. As for Kathryn—she would have no motive at all. She was a successful career woman who graciously helped provide for her stepmother's needs by buying her medication.

I refused to suspect Brandy, although she was capable of such an act, as she had proved today. Who else was there? Until I had won the little girl's confidence completely, I knew I couldn't ask her.

Worry nagged at me. Who wanted Aunt Corrie out of the way badly enough to push her down the stairs? I must stay and keep an eye on her. There was no other way.

I remained in my room most of the day, writing letters and arranging my summer. I had planned to go on the Caribbean cruise in order to sort out my thoughts regarding Eric. Although he wrote me faithfully and always expressed his deep love for me, I still was filled with doubts concerning our future relationships.

Eric was begging me to see him before going on the cruise. But with conditions so unsettled at Meriweather Hall, and especially with Aunt Corinda, I knew I couldn't leave. I spent a rather awkward hour writing a letter to cancel my reservations for the trip. I'd lose most of my deposit, but at this point remaining with my great-aunt was far more important.

I took out a clean sheet and wrote to Eric. "I can't think of leaving her now," I told him. "There are too many unanswered questions, too much of a tension-charged atmosphere."

The warm afternoon wheeled slowly to a close, and it was time I dressed for dinner. I knew Paul would be there but I didn't know about Colin or Kathryn. Sometimes they dropped in unexpectedly at the last minute.

After I donned a cool, green sleeveless shift, I put a fresh Band-Aid on my forehead and brushed my brown hair into a wing over my left eyebrow, partly trying to hide the patch.

Already I heard Annie Jane bring up the trays for Mrs. Crosby and Aunt Corrie, and I knew dinner would soon be ready.

Feeling a bit creaky as I walked down the stairs, I realized I was using muscles that had apparently taken a beating from my fall. Grabbing the newel post at the bottom of the stairs, I clenched my teeth to get a grip on myself when Brandy bounded down the steps behind me. She had changed from her grimy denim playsuit into a clean pink-checked dress, most likely upon Annie Jane's firm orders.

She eyed me sharply and immediately spotted my bandage.

"You gonna tell my daddy what happened?" she said, her green eyes wary. "I didn't make you fall. I thought I saw a rat and wanted to push you out of the way."

I smiled feebly, not believing her for a minute. Reaching out my hand, I laid it on her shoulder.

"That was thoughtful of you. No. I won't mention it to your father."

"I think Snow White likes you," Brandy chattered, probably trying to mend a few fences as well as to keep my mind away from the event.

"How about that!" I exclaimed. "I'm flattered. Well, I like Snow White too. She's a special cat."

"You think so?"

"Oh, definitely."

"Well, I guess she is."

Paul came out of the downstairs bathroom at that moment. The tired lines of his face seemed to have deepened, but he apparently noticed my bandage in spite of my efforts to cover it up.

"What's happened, Amy?" he asked, his voice full of concern. "Your forehead. . . ."

"Brandy and I were in the horse barn tangling with Thomasina's latest brood. I . . . got too close to one of the stalls and fell against it. It's nothing."

"I hope not."

He pulled a paper sack from his pocket and handed it to me. "Here, Amy. It's for you."

"What is it?"

"Open it and see."

I took a small carton from the sack and stared at it. "Why, it's *Moon Song,* my favorite perfume. How'd you know?"

"I didn't. You said Brandy smashed your bottle, and I decided to replace it. It—it was Sue's favorite."

Numbly I slipped it back into the sack and tucked it into my pocket. "Th-thank you, Paul. I appreciate the gesture." Somehow my heart wasn't in it. Naturally he would remember only *Moon Song* because it was the brand he'd bought for his wife.

We walked into the small dining room and sat down at the table. As Annie Jane served the delicious sweet corn and fried chicken, the meal passed pleasantly. Even Brandy seemed on her best behavior, probably trying to cover up the awkward situation of my fall from the loft earlier.

73

She left the table as soon as she had finished the chocolate pudding dessert. Paul and I lingered over our coffee.

"Brandy seems to be shaping up a little. Have you noticed?" he said, a hint of eagerness in his tired voice.

I stirred the coffee with a spoon before I sipped it. "Oh, yes. At least, I think she's getting there."

"Is she still giving you trouble?"

I sipped my coffee slowly and set down the cup in the saucer. "We're making progress. Maybe Snow White will do the trick."

"Oh. You mean the white kitten."

Laughing, I clinked the spoon idly against the saucer. "Yes. You could be right. I've prayed that she'll respond to me somehow."

We were both quiet for a long minute. Then Paul asked—guardedly, I thought: "How was Corrie-Mom today?"

"She—she showed no response this morning, the way she did yesterday. Oh, Paul, if only she'd continue to improve. I want so much to talk to her, really talk. Maybe she'll give us some answers."

Paul looked at me sharply. "Answers to what?" he said a trifle harshly.

"If she were pushed down the stairs—"

"You still harping on that?" he cut in angrily. "She slipped and fell, and that's all there's to it!"

I turned an icy gaze on the intense, dark young man who sat across the table from me.

"Maybe she did. But if she was pushed, it was because someone wanted her out of the way. And we need to know who that someone is."

He rose abruptly from the table and started for the door. Then he whirled around. "Okay, Amy. Let's you and me go

74

upstairs right now and see how near—or how far—she is coming out of her condition." He waited for me in the doorway.

"That's a good idea." I got to my feet rather stiffly, still feeling the bruises of the morning, brushed past Paul, and started for the hall.

He swung in behind me and we walked up the stairs without a word. At his knock on Aunt Corrie's door, Mrs. Crosby opened it.

"Well?" she growled.

"We'd like to see Mrs. Ward, please," he said, his voice still hard.

Frowning, the nurse flung open the door and stood aside as we stepped into the dimly lit room.

I moved ahead of Paul and hurried to the bed. Aunt Corrie's eyes seemed hooded, and I laid my hand gently on the white forehead.

"Aunt Corrie, it's me—Amy. Paul's here too. Can you open your eyes?"

Then I noticed that the lids were only half-closed. Yet the look in the pale blue eyes was dull and glassy. There was absolutely no response.

10

Stunned, I walked from the room. Never had I seen the glazed, dull look on my aunt's face before. She had appeared to be asleep but now it was as though she was—*drugged*. I knew she received a liquid medication from the doctor, for I had seen the brown bottle on the bedside stand in her room. I also knew Kathryn took the vial faithfully to have it refilled. According to the label it was a liquid vitamin supplement to be administered twice daily. To take medication when it was necessary was one thing; to be doped was another.

I decided not to mention my suspicion to Paul, for I wasn't sure if he had noticed her dazed, half-open eyes.

He looked grim when we stepped into the hall, and I saw a frown crease his brow as he laid a hand on my arm.

"Well, Amy, Corrie-Mom looks farther than ever from making strides to recovery, as you seem to think," he said in a cynical voice I had grown to loathe.

I flung off his grip. "She—she looks far away tonight," I said brusquely. "But yesterday she—I know she realized I was there. Her gaze was as clear and candid as yours is right now!"

"I'm sorry, Amy. I've tried to warn you not to get your hopes up. She's been hurt more seriously than you seem to think. You can't expect—"

"Maybe," I said, my voice icy, "just maybe she will come out of this. I have faith that she will."

"You and your faith! You saw her tonight. If she looks to you as though. . . ."

I wasn't listening. If Paul and Colin and Kathryn all refused to believe that the Lord might choose to restore Corinda Ward, that was their business. I was going to hang onto my faith that she could recover. None of them had seen her yesterday as I had. I couldn't forget the look of recognition in her eyes.

Back in my room, I sat down in my rocker and pondered the situation. Was it possible I expected too much? That she was, as Paul pointed out, hurt far more seriously than we had perhaps thought? If so, why had she seemed to respond in some vague sense for days when I had read to her, and now appeared to be in a drugged stupor?"

I prayed hard and long that night, pleading with the Lord to allow her to recover, if it were his will.

"But if it isn't your will, Lord," I added, "it's okay too. I just don't want to see her lying like a corpse without any recognition in her eyes!"

I slept more soundly than I thought possible and awoke to the sound of sharp pellets of rain flinging themselves against my windows. I got up and gazed out at the shiny plastic curtain that seemed to be pulled over the world.

Dressing quickly, I went down to breakfast, which I ate at the big kitchen table since I knew Paul left for work early. Brandy was nowhere in sight. I wasn't as stiff as I had expected, and the cut on my forehead was only a trifle sore.

I had formed the habit of breakfasting alone, even preparing my own meal. Hot oatmeal and buttered whole

77

wheat toast with juice and coffee had become my standard breakfast menu.

More often than not, Annie Jane was out, either cleaning or waiting to bring down Mrs. Crosby's breakfast tray. I expected mere tolerance from Annie Jane, although she had treated me warmly as a child. She had, in fact, almost spoiled me when I visited Meriweather Hall in those earlier years.

I used to help her bake oatmeal cookies, spooning globs of tan-colored moist dough onto sturdy tin cookie sheets. She used to cluck, I remember, when I smeared bits of dough over the pan.

"That ain't no way to do it, child!" she fumed. Yet she always allowed me to help.

Time had taken its toll of both her strength and patience, yet I was sure she wasn't ready to relinquish her position in the old brick house. She still felt responsible for "Miz Ward."

I washed up my bowl and spoon and put the dishes away in the roomy white cupboards. I had planned to work in the garden today, but with the rain drumming steadily on the windows it was out of the question.

At a sound behind me, I turned. Brandy stood in the doorway, her hair still tousled from sleep. Her clean playsuit was buttoned incorrectly, but I made no comment.

"Well, how will you spend your day?" I asked as brightly as I could without sounding facetious.

"Yuck!" she sputtered. "I'd go play with Thomasina's kittens if it wasn't for this nasty rain."

She glanced briefly at my forehead and probably noticed the Band-Aid was gone. Her eyes, although not happy, weren't stony. Of course, Brandy's mood swings were often swift and unpredictable.

"Maybe we can take a saucer of milk to the barn later," I said.

"Thomasina's good about catching mice and birds," Brandy informed me wisely, browsing in the pantry for dry cereal.

"Need my help?" I asked, waiting at one end of the table.

"No. I mix up what I want," she said nonchalantly, dumping a few kernels and flakes of this and that into her bowl. "What kind do you like best?" she asked, pouring the rich creamy milk over the cereal. It popped and crackled.

"I cook my own oatmeal," I said. "It's good for a person."

"Yuck!" she spat out, drizzling a heaping teaspoon of sugar over the bowl.

I watched her silently for several seconds, then started for the door. "I'll be upstairs if you need me."

"I don't need you!" she flung out, and I could almost see the green eyes harden.

"Okay," I said nonchalantly. "Suit yourself."

She gave me a hard look, then turned away.

As I came upstairs Annie Jane pattered out of the sickroom with the breakfast tray. Mrs. Crosby stood in the doorway.

"Oh, Mrs. Crosby," I called out. "May I speak to you for a minute?"

She nodded at Annie Jane, who left with the empty bowls and remained large and aloof in the doorway.

"Well?"

I had become accustomed to her gruff word of disapproval but decided not to let it bother me.

"Mrs. Crosby, when Paul and I dropped in on my great-

aunt last night, she looked as though she'd been—doped
. . . drugged. Her eyes were dull and glazed. . . ."

The woman seemed to grow bigger and more formidable
as she stood in front of me, almost filling the doorway. She
placed her hands on her ample hips and glowered.

"How dare you suggest that I sedate my patient!"

"I'm not accusing you, Mrs. Crosby," I said, trying to pla-
cate her. "It's not what I meant. I only wondered—"

"Well, you're wrong. I give her the medicine her doctor
prescribes. I wouldn't dare overstep his orders and give
her somethin' else."

The door slammed in my face. I stood in the hall, facing
the door, and felt as though an iron gate had been locked
in front of me. I had the distinct feeling that *someone* was
trying to keep Aunt Corrie from waking up to tell what she
knew.

Slowly I turned to my room, deeply disturbed. If only I
knew what was going on. Should I try to read to Aunt Corrie this morning? Perhaps it was the gray gloom outdoors,
or maybe it was my own restless mood, but I had no desire
to see my great-aunt in the state of stupor she'd seemingly
been in last night.

Walking up to the windows, I pulled back the dull green
drapes as far as I could. Rain still drummed intermittently
against the brick walls of the old house, and a small sharp
gust of wind swished the wet drops against the window-
panes and thrust clammy fingers around the edges of glass.
A tendril of ivy twisted on the brick wall and clung to the
window frame. The trees were dark silhouettes against the
gray sky, and I shivered in the chilly dampness of the
morning.

The day seemed to close in on me and I yearned to get

away from Meriweather Hall and its secretive, haunting mysteries. I was almost sorry I had canceled my trip to the Caribbean. Right now I needed the calm blue seas and the slow steady creak of the cruise ship to make me forget the puzzling intrigue that seemed to taunt me here. I almost felt like calling Eric and telling him that I needed him. That I was coming back to marry him. I'd leave Meriweather Hall and its baffling questions behind me forever and forget all that bothered me here.

That would be the easiest way out of my dilemma. Yet the problem would not be solved, and I knew I could never rest until it was.

A sudden thought hit me. Perhaps Aunt Corrie's doctor could help. He might tell me if there had been a change in the prescription to account for her sedated condition.

I moved swiftly from the window and went to my closet. Rummaging through my clothes, I pulled out the soft dove-gray slacks and delicate gray-and-mauve toned top and slipped the raincoat from its hanger.

In a few minutes I had changed, grabbed my purse and car keys, and hurried down the stairs. Brandy was curled up on the front porch, holding out her hands and trying to catch the big drops that ran down the colonnades.

"Amy! You going away?" she asked, her voice anxious.

"I must go to town on business," I said, starting down the steps hurriedly. She was behind me, pulling on my arm.

"You'll come back, won't you?"

I looked at her. Unpredictable child. Yesterday she had dared me to go away. The green eyes were soft, gentle. I smiled. "Of course, I'll be back. Tell Annie Jane I'll bring along some milk and a frying chicken, will you?"

She moved back and nodded. "Sure. Don't be too long, Amy."

I hurried to the double garage, backed my Honda out, then made a turn toward the short graveled drive and spun in the soft wet dirt. My wipers swished steadily as I turned onto the blacktop. Blobs of water made erratic patterns on the road in front of me, and tires hissed. and splashed as cars passed.

The name of Aunt Corrie's doctor was Henry Blair, I had learned from the medicine bottle. The telephone directory listed his office in the Waylan Clinic.

After a few detours and wrong turns I spotted the building and left my car in the ample parking space beside it. The clinic was built of buff brick, with wide, glass-paned doors and low, overhanging eaves that dripped from the rain.

Stepping inside, I told the pert, dark-haired receptionist what I wanted.

"Dr. Blair has a busy schedule," she told me, "but if you're only asking a question, I think he can see you after he is finished with a patient. Please sit down and wait."

I took a chair, picked up a magazine, paged through it hastily, then looked around. The clinic looked opulent, and I was sure Dr. Blair had a thriving practice. Several other patients waited, some restless, others engrossed in their reading materials.

It wasn't long until the receptionist called my name and motioned me to the door that led to the suite of offices and examining rooms. Dr. Blair was seated behind a desk in the consulting room, a thin, gray man who smiled to show a set of even white teeth.

"Miss Sutton?" he asked, rising to his feet. "What may I

do for you?" He motioned me to a soft chair as he sat down again.

"I'm Corinda Ward's grandniece and I've come to stay at Meriweather Hall for the summer," I said by way of introduction.

"Oh, yes, of course. What seems to be the problem there?"

I hesitated. The doctor seemed amicable enough, but I sensed an aloofness, a haughtiness which might be his professional air. Yet I couldn't be sure. He leaned back in his chair and waited.

"I wondered why my great-aunt suddenly seems drugged," I plunged in. "Is she on a new medication? Why should she—"

"She is receiving the same medication I prescribed for her when she left the hospital," he said. "You say, she appears to be drugged?"

"Yes, I do,'" and I told him of my experience with Aunt Corrie. "Suddenly she has a glazed, dull look in her eyes. As though—"

"You must be mistaken," he cut in coldly. "What I am giving her will not keep her in a stupor. Rather, the vitamins will help her come out of it."

"Is there a chance Aunt Corrie can come out of this completely?" I asked, trying to penetrate the man's austere manner.

He tapped his finger on the desk, then abruptly got up. "It's possible but quite unlikely," he said in a tone that dismissed me. As if on cue his nurse appeared and ushered me out the door.

The rain still blew from gray skies as I walked to my car. I hadn't received a scrap of information, and his words shook me up. I felt hemmed in, as though there was a secret conspiracy to keep me from the truth, to drive me away from Meriweather Hall.

I got into my Honda, backed out of the parking place, and pulled back onto the wet, shiny avenue again. Rain and tears made a sort of kaleidoscope of moving traffic as I drove down the long, shimmering vista of wet streets.

I brought a few groceries from town and parked my car in the garage at Meriweather Hall. Then I hurried into the house, put the food in the refrigerator, and started up the stairs. I caught a glimpse of Brandy curled up before the TV in the library, so I didn't stop to talk. I took off my wet raincoat and draped it on a hanger to dry.

When I came into my room the strong scent of *Moon Song* drifted to my nostrils. The perfume bottle Paul had given me lay shattered on the rug. Anger surged through me when I realized Brandy was the cause of it. When would the child learn that she must respect the property of others?

It was Sue's favorite. I couldn't escape Paul's words. Of course, Brandy would resent anyone else using the same brand as her mother's. But it still didn't give her license to destroy.

I went back downstairs to the library. Brandy was sprawled on her stomach, her bare legs kicking. Marching to the TV, I switched it off.

"Hey, Amy!" she protested, looking up. "The cartoons weren't over. Why'd you switch off the TV?"

I held the shattered bottle out to her on a crumpled tissue. *"That's* why. What do you mean, destroying other people's property?" I demanded.

She sat up and hugged her knees, and I saw the hard

84

glints creep back into her eyes. "You shouldn't use the same kind of perfume as my Momma," she said sullenly. "Don't you know that?"

"No, I don't and what's more, I have the right to use whatever perfume I wish. As for you, young lady, you're old enough to know that you've no right to destroy what isn't yours. Is that clear?"

Without a word, she scrambled to her feet and rushed out of the room.

I sighed. Maybe she felt threatened by my using the same brand of perfume as her mother. Still, she needed discipline. But I decided not to pursue the matter further. Perhaps she would remember next time. Of course, with Brandy one never knew.

Better check on Aunt Corrie, I decided. I hadn't had my special time with her this morning and hadn't seen her since yesterday. Perhaps today she was more alert.

I picked up my Bible and rapped sharply on the door across the hall. After what seemed like an interminable time I heard Mrs. Crosby's heavy footsteps as she moved toward the door.

When she opened it I tried to push into the room, but she barred my way.

"Your aunt's runnin' a fever," she said gruffly. "No one comes and goes but Annie Jane with the trays and Kathryn with the medicine!" Then she slammed the door.

Stunned, I turned away. Fever? What was wrong with Aunt Corrie *now*?

11

With a deep sigh I returned to my room, feeling troubled and suddenly weary. I dropped into my rocker and stared out of the window.

The rain had let up and a pale light bathed the landscape that stretched around the hall, casting a strange greenness to the unkempt lawns and the meadow beyond the yard. I opened the window and breathed the sweet, damp air. From the trees came the stitch-stitch-stitch of insects sewing their endless chants. Bunches of thick gray clouds trailed after the rain like stray sheep, and each shallow pool in the driveway held a patch of sky.

I glanced at my watch. It was lunchtime, but I wasn't hungry. I had honestly felt Aunt Corinda was gaining health and strength, but now she had a fever on top of the dull, glazed look in her eyes. . . .

"Dear Lord," I prayed, "I don't know what the future holds for her. But please let her know, somehow, that she isn't alone. That I'm here . . . and that you are always with her. . . ."

Feeling somewhat relieved, I went downstairs to lunch. Brandy waited for me in the kitchen, a large bowl of thick, creamy tomato soup in front of her.

"So you did come back," she greeted me nonchalantly, as though our sharp exchange at the TV had never happened.

I had almost forgotten about the moody little child in my own preoccupation. She must've been afraid I was going away for good and she would be bereft again.

"As soon as the rain stopped, I fed the cats," she went on, ignoring my silence.

I dipped a bowlful of soup for myself and sat down at the large white table across from her. "Good! And how's Thomasina's family?"

"Frisky. They all tumbled from the hayloft, and guess what they're doing now?" she asked, her green eyes alive with excitement.

I pretended to scratch my head in thought. "Oh, I'm sure I couldn't guess in a million years. What are they up to now?"

"They're playing on the grass under the swing."

"Are they, now? And how's Snow White?" I asked between sips of the tasty soup.

Suddenly a frown tugged at Brandy's mouth and her green eyes hardened. "You didn't even want to feed her, and you said you would! You blasted away in your car, and when you came back you shut yourself up in your room!"

"I'm so sorry, Brandy," I said, shaking my head. "I had to go to town on an errand. When I came back . . . I wanted to see Grandma Corrie, to read to her from the Bible. But. . . ." I sighed again.

"Well, why didn't you feed the cats? You promised!"

"Brandy, Mrs. Crosby tells me Grandma Corrie has a fever. She didn't even let me in to see her. I guess I felt pretty bad about it and forgot everything else."

Her stormy look softened. "If you pray for her, she'll get better, won't she?"

The question caught me off guard. It wasn't easy to answer. For how can a child understand that God's ways aren't always our ways? I took a deep breath.

"I hope she will, Brandy. But we have to remember that God's ways are best. Yes, I'll pray, we'll both pray. But let's keep in mind that we must accept whatever God chooses."

She seemed to listen intently. Then I noticed the stony look creep back into her eyes. She jumped, almost upsetting the leftover dregs of soup in her bowl, and fled from the kitchen without a word.

My heart ached for the troubled little girl. Surely she must feel lonely and forsaken. First, her own mother taken ill. Then Grandma Corrie's fall, and her hopes for recovery dashed—especially if what she claimed she saw was true, that Grandma Corrie was pushed. And I hadn't made things any easier by ignoring her. Somehow I wasn't capable of coping with all my problems today.

I spend most of the afternoon in my room, puttering with needless little jobs like filing my nails, plucking my eyebrows, and washing and setting my hair. They were all gestures of frustration and boredom. I tried to corral my thoughts, but somehow I couldn't fully concentrate.

When I heard Paul's car pull into the drive, I patted on the last bit of makeup and hurried downstairs. I had reached the hall when I heard his footsteps on the front porch.

Brandy flew into her father's arms the minute he stepped through the door.

"Daddy—Daddy!" she shrieked. "Oh, my daddy. Please—please don't *ever* go away and leave me!"

He stroked the reddish hair gently and whispered audibly in her ear. "No, Brandy. Of course, I won't leave you."

"But if Grandma Corrie dies, Amy will go away. I—I don't want to be here alone."

Paul kissed her, then carried her into the library, motioning for me to follow. He drew her onto his lap as he seated himself on the sofa. Then he turned to me. I sat down in the brown chair and waited.

"Now what's this about Grandma Corrie dying?" he asked both of us.

Brandy pointed to me. "You tell him."

"I learned this morning," I began quietly, "that she has a fever. Mrs. Crosby refused to let me in to see her."

"And Amy says maybe God won't make her better. Just like Momma!"

Paul glanced from Brandy to me, and I dropped my gaze.

"Paul. . . ," I began slowly, "it's hard to believe just after she had begun to make progress. I couldn't tell Brandy that everything was going to be peachy."

"But just after I told her I was sorry about breaking the vase and everything!" Brandy went on hotly. "I thought God would . . . let her stay with us. And—and Amy too."

I caught Paul's look, and saw the pain, the sadness in his eyes. He had been my hero, the one person I adored as a child that summer twelve years ago. Yet, when I craved fun and laughter I always had Colin. It was still that way.

Just at that moment Annie Jane stepped into the doorway. "Brandy, you better look after your cats. They's climbin' all over the stone fence. Soon they's gonna scoot and disappear."

Brandy jumped from her father's arms. "I'd better put them back in the barn." In a flash she was gone from the room.

Annie Jane shook her head, muttered something unintelligible, and left. I started to get up too, but Paul waved me down.

"Please stay, Amy. We need to talk."

Settling back into my chair, I folded my hands on my knees and waited. What was on Paul's mind?

"Amy, I know you've been here for five weeks, and in all that time we haven't really had a chance to talk. I know I've tried several times, but it hasn't been easy for me . . . to tell you how I feel toward Corrie-Mom. You may have wondered."

All the bitterness I had seen in the past weeks seemed to have drained from his face, and I saw only unabashed love. Drawing a deep breath, I leaned forward.

"Go on," I said.

"Our mother died when I was ten, too young to be left without a mother. Dad did his best with us kids, but I'm sure it wasn't easy for him. I think I know how Brandy must feel . . . alone and forsaken. But when Dad met your great-aunt—I know she was somewhat older than he was —we really fell for her. At least, I know I did. I was already fourteen when they were married. She—she was like a real mother to me, to all of us. She—she was really special. I remember the time I had my motorcycle accident. I wasn't hurt, but Dad was furious. He said I'd been reckless, a poor model for Colin and Kathryn. Being the oldest I was always expected to be an example. It just happened, I guess. One of those things. Corrie-Mom helped me to see that everyone makes mistakes. There were other times like that."

He grew silent. I could see this intense dark young boy, yearning for love, for understanding, and finding it in his stepmother.

"When I fell in love with Susan Riley, Dad was against our marriage from the first, especially because we were both so young," he went on. "I already knew Sue had a physical problem, but we loved each other and got married in spite of it. Yet through all of that Corrie-Mom smiled and cheered and remained our friend. After Dad died, Colin and Kathryn seemed to draw away from her, but somehow I couldn't. She was still special. Brandy was her granddaughter just as surely as if she'd been her blood kin.

"As Sue's illness worsened, Corrie-Mom insisted on helping. She paid some of my staggering medical bills. They seemed out of reach for me to manage, especially since Sue's condition worsened suddenly and I was forced to take her to the Connor Clinic. It's quite far out, but it's the cheapest place I could find. That's when Corrie-Mom insisted Brandy and I move back with her here in Meriweather Hall. She knew how badly I needed help, in maintaining a home and with Brandy. After her accident—oh, Amy can't you see how it shook me up? How I can't let myself *dare* hope for better things? I just pray she makes it."

His voice broke, and I sensed the sob deep inside of him. His heart, so full of love for family, was still the same tender, gentle Paul I had always known. Stripped of his bitterness, he was vulnerable, compassionate—and very dear.

I caught myself sharply. *Am I falling in love with Paul Ward?* But it's so wrong. He doesn't share my faith, and he deeply loves his gravely ill wife.

Help me to be strong, Lord, I prayed silently. Help me to do what's right. Let me love Eric enough to marry him. . . . Yet deep in my heart I wondered if I ever could.

12

The NO ADMITTANCE sign on Aunt Corrie's bedroom door the next morning kept me at a distance. Once when I knocked to ask about her, the big brawny nurse angrily ordered me away.

"I got more to do than give out medical reports," she fumed.

When I caught Annie Jane coming out of the sickroom with the breakfast tray, I laid a hand on her arm.

"Please tell me, Annie Jane," I said in a quiet voice, "how is my great-aunt?"

The elderly housekeeper looked at me with a flash of her old sensitivity. "She's not eatin' good. That's all I know."

"But does she seem—very ill?"

She shook her head. "I can't say, Miss Amy. She was a tossin' a lot just now. Not quiet like the way she's been."

With that, she shuffled down the hall with her tray, and I returned to my room.

I usually helped Annie Jane with cleaning on Fridays, but she had told me at breakfast that she didn't think we should make noises with the buzzing vacuum. Although I was certain the whirr wouldn't bother Aunt Corrie, I didn't say so. I'd discovered it was best to humor the woman. It made for better relations.

In my room, I opened the windows wide to the bright

morning sunshine. A blazing wedge of sunlight caught in the mirror of my dressing table like an unshafted sword, and I went to pull the drapes. High cauliflower clouds seemed to hang in the blue sky without movement, their curded bases dropping patches of shade upon the ground below.

I sat down in my rocker and poured out my heart in prayer. I felt so helpless, so unneeded. I truly wanted just to be with my great-aunt and perhaps let her sense that I was there. If my presence would calm her, I was willing to do nothing but sit beside her bed.

After an hour of restless praying, pacing, and thinking, I realized I needed activity and decided to clean the upstairs hall closet.

When I'd gone to look for an extra fan one day, I'd almost choked on dust and cobwebs that sifted from the small, crowded storage closet. I wouldn't dispose of anything valuable, of course, but if I wiped the dust and restacked the contents it would give me something to do and the closet would be clean as well.

I went down to the kitchen for the small stepstool Annie Jane kept near the kitchen cabinets so she could reach the top shelves.

"May I borrow this for about an hour?" I asked as the elderly woman shuffled into the room with the inevitable tray in her hands.

"What do you need it for?"

"That upstairs hall closet is so cluttered I can't find anything," I said. "I'll just clean out the dust and stack everything back neatly."

"Just don't you dump anything out, Miss Amy," she grouched.

"Oh, I shan't. But the place is a disaster," I called out over my shoulder as I hurried back upstairs.

First I moved out the things that hampered my work and piled them into the hall. There were boxes of Christmas tree ornaments, old magazines, musty journals, worn scruffy shoes, and floppy tattered straw hats, not to mention old clothes. The closet apparently hadn't been touched in years, except to shove more things into it.

The dust that sifted from the shelves was stifling. I brushed them thoroughly before restacking the contents.

"If I had my way, I'd junk half the stuff," I muttered under my breath.

"What did you say, Amy?" Brandy spoke behind me.

I turned around, and she burst into laughter.

"Oh, Amy, do you know you've got dirty smudges all over your cheeks?"

I screwed up my face. "Well, of course. I'm the old woman in the shoe. I've got so much junk I don't know what to do!"

"Can I play with those old shoes and one of those floppy hats?"

I peered at the disarray on the hall floor and sighed. "Well, why not? It gives me less junk to pile back in." I gave the top shelf another swipe with my dust cloth and heard Brandy sifting through the clutter on the floor. Then she drew her breath sharply.

"What's this, Amy? Sure looks like scribbly writing."

She held up several musty gray journals, and I reached out one hand. "Let me see."

Straddling the stepstool I paged through the crisp yellow leaves. I recognized them as notes my great-grandfather Meriweather had made pertaining to his mines. The old notes might prove interesting.

94

Brandy had lost interest and had gone off to her room with her collection of hats and shoes as I browsed through the pale, scrawled pages. A few faded yellow envelopes spilled from the journal. I slid them back into the book and continued to leaf through it, scanning the scribbled notes at random.

"Old No. 2 good producer. Get another two men on job."

"Looks like No. 6 has had it. Will have to shut it down soon."

"No. 4 shaft cave-in. Get Herb to clear it out."

"Made entrance on No. 2 inside of hill for drift but need vertical shaft for removal. . . ."

There was nothing here that really interested me. I closed the old journals, dusted them, and replaced them on the shelves. Half an hour later I had finished the job and headed for the shower. At least one spot in the old mansion was squeaky clean today.

Then I tackled the upstairs bathroom, scouring and waxing the lavatory and tub. I changed the towels and wiped the tiled floor.

As I sauntered along the hall, hoping for some word from Aunt Corrie's room, I heard a sound behind me and turned. Kathryn came from the sickroom, her movements quick and birdlike.

"Kathryn?" I called out when she would've passed by me without a word. "How's Aunt Corrie?" It wasn't like her to ignore me.

She paused a little, looked at me, and her gaze quickly darted away. Then she began to move on.

"Look, what's going on?" I demanded sharply, grabbing her arm. "That's my great-aunt in there. I have a right to know what's happening!"

With a swiftly drawn breath she shook her head a little. "I can't say. I'm sorry, but she seems restless and Crosby says to send for Dr. Blair. I told her to give her another dose of medicine, but she says she won't do that without doctor's orders. I thought Corrie-Mom was doing better lately, but now—" She brushed past me and headed for the stairs. "I'd better call the doctor quick."

I watched the neat, slim-skirted figure hurry away. So the doctor was being called. I was grateful that Mrs. Crosby, for all her brusqueness, was following the doctor's orders about the medication, and thankful for Kathryn's obvious concern.

About to return to my room, I noticed Brandy standing in the doorway of her room, cuddling Snow White in her arms.

"Brandy!" I snapped. "What are you doing with the cats in the house? I thought Annie Jane said—"

"It's not her house. It's ours!" she pouted, stroking the white fur gently. "Besides, I have only Snow White here. The rest are shut up in the barn. You said she was special."

She swaggered toward me as though daring me to snatch the kitten away from her to take it to the barn. Her green eyes were bright and glinting.

"Besides," she went on blithely, "I bet you had cats when you were little."

Now she's trying to appeal to my empathy, I thought.

"Only when I had permission to do so," I said shortly.

A tear glistened in her eyes and stole down her cheeks. She swung around fiercely. "You don't love me anymore, Amy!" she cried.

I hurried after her and cupped her quivering chin in my palm. "Oh, Brandy, that's not so. Why do you say that?"

" 'Cause you don't talk nice to me."

"Come with me." I took her arm, led her to my room, and closed the door. She set the squirmy little kitten on the floor. I sat down beside her on the edge of the bed.

"Look, Brandy, I'm sorry if I was short with you, but you know Grandma Corrie's very sick. I guess I was thinking about her, and that makes me feel bad."

She nodded so hard her red hair bobbed into her neck. "I know. But aren't we gonna pray for her? I thought you said God—"

"Of course, we'll pray," I cut in. "Let's bow our heads right now."

I was amazed at her simple, trusting, childlike prayer. I thought, If *she* has faith for Aunt Corrie's healing, why shouldn't I?

After we got up from the bed, I scooped up Snow White, who was swiping at the crumpled pink tissues in my wastebasket.

"After lunch you and I will take a long walk to Old Number Two. Would you like that?" I asked.

"Oh, yes, I would. Can we take Snow White with us?"

"We'll see. We don't want her to get away, do we?"

"I'll hold onto her real tight."

"Maybe you'd better leave her home. But tell you what, for now, why not take her out to play with Minnie and Mousie and Mozzarella."

"You're silly! she giggled. "It's Cheesey!"

"Well, I came close, didn't I?" I pretended chagrin.

She laughed again, and with a skip and a run she was off toward the back stairs.

I started down the front stairs to see if I could help Annie Jane when the doorbell rang. Dr. Blair stood in the doorway when I opened it and let him in.

"I understand Mrs. Ward is ill," he said perfunctorily. Doubtless he was a man of few words, as I'd discovered only the day before.

"Yes, she is. Please follow me."

I led him up the stairs and showed him to her room. More than anything I wanted to follow him in, to see for myself how my aunt was. But I doubted that he would allow it.

I'd waylay him on his way out, I decided. Perhaps he would have more heartening news for us.

But I was in the kitchen fixing sandwiches for lunch when I heard the front door close, and before I could run after him, Brandy stormed through the back door.

"Snow White was awful hungry," she panted. "I guess it's time for her lunch now."

"And for ours too," I said.

I heard noises in the back part of the house and knew Annie Jane had begun with her cleaning after all.

Trying to make the noon meal a happy time, I sang some jolly little tunes I had taught my fifth-graders:

> Alice the camel has . . . ten humps; Alice the camel has . . . ten humps . . . ten humps, so go, Alice, go! Boom! Boom! Boom!

For the first time in weeks I felt completely at ease with Brandy Ward. In spite of her rather unpredictable responses, I felt she had begun to trust me. Perhaps her resentment toward me was fading.

We had just downed our sandwiches, sliced tomatoes, and iced cocoa when Colin blew in like a refreshing summer breeze.

"Well, look who's here," he shouted, kissing first Brandy, then grabbing me for a more ardent, longer-lasting peck.

Laughing, I pulled away from him. "You know, you're just in time for a walk. That is, if you want to get away from the smell of all that filthy lucre for awhile."

"It's my afternoon off," he said, "so I said to myself, 'I just know Meriweather Hall is dying for a sight of me,' and so here I am." He grinned boyishly and threw out his arms wide. "But what's this about a walk?"

"Do you realize, Colin Ward, that I haven't been down to Old Number Two since I got here? You always take me to ritzy restaurants to eat, but I'm dying for a glimpse of our old hangout," I parried. "Besides, I promised Brandy she and I would stretch our legs. Too much TV and sitting around makes Jill a dull girl."

"Lead on, MacSutton," Colin droned in a hollow monotone.

The three of us went out the back door, then cut across the broad yard where a wooden gate opened to the meadow that lay to the east. Brandy had decided against taking Snow White, for she feared her pet might run down into the old abandoned mine.

A narrow lane had served as an access road that led to the nearest of Great-grandpa's lead and zinc mines. Years ago when the mines had flourished, he had employed a good many Waylan men. But finally the ore had given out, and some of the mines were abandoned. He had sold his other mines when his heart began to fail and he was forced to give up the responsibility of managing them. By then he had amassed a considerable fortune. I had heard the story often from my mother, his only grandchild.

This mine where we were now headed lay more than a

half mile away. My mother remembered when it was still functioning and how the miners went down into the ground through a vertical shaft. But since it had been abandoned the adit had been boarded up.

The rocky, hilly land farther east was pockmarked with other abandoned mines. When the ore gave out, the miners simply moved out and left. Old Number Two lay nearest the Meriweather property.

We walked along the road, now weed-grown, skirted on either side by a sweet hay-filled meadow.

"Who harvests all this good-smelling hay these days?" I asked Colin as we ambled along the slightly muddy path. Brandy skipped ahead, chasing butterflies and picking up brightly colored pebbles.

"Corrie-Mom sold it ages ago," Colin said, swinging his arms briskly as he walked. "After she gave up the horses, there was no more need for hay, of course, and farmers were happy for it. But we still used the old road for hikes."

I heard a slight sound behind me and saw a flash of white. It was Brandy's favorite kitten.

"Brandy!" I called out. "Look who's following us!"

"Snow White!" she squealed, chasing the white bit of fluff until she caught it. "You naughty little thing. What are you doing here?"

Prattling to her kitten, she trotted ahead of us. The path grew more hilly as it crept eastward. The building that had once housed mining equipment was no longer beside the road, and only a few limestone rocks jutted out of the high weeds. Healing grass had long reclaimed the spot where the building once stood. The big cottonwood I had remembered, stretched gaunt and dry, nothing more than a dead skeleton. I thought, old paths smother under the weeds, and open mines may have its starts buried, yet the truth my loved ones taught me lives on, ageless, irrefutable, and changeless as these zinc-ribbed hills. . . .

We had reached the mine-site entrance. Debris and rocks cluttered around the boarded-up opening in the ground. As Brandy ran up to the very edge, Colin called out sharply,

"Be careful, Brandy. The ground won't be solid, after that big rain."

She backed away, holding onto the squirming kitten. We stood for awhile, silent in the warm afternoon, and surveyed the spot which had once bustled with activity. I tried to picture the scene, the trucks and carts filled with ore, crawling down the old access road toward the refinery in town.

"This must have been quite a big deal once," I said, thinking of Great-grandpa Meriweather as the hub of all the activity and remembering his stories. "Time has swallowed up so much of the past."

Colin took my elbow lightly. "Yes, but are we the better for it?" he mused idly.

"As long as we don't forget the lessons we've learned."

"Come now, Amy," he said with a quick, dry laugh, "don't sound so morbid. I know you're thinking of Corrie-Mom, but what's happened has happened. Neither you nor I can change that."

"Maybe not. But if we can do something about the circumstances—"

"Fiddlesticks! What's done is done. You're getting entirely too obsessed with the situation. Besides, all your so-called evidence is circumstantial. For one afternoon please forget Meriweather Hall and have some fun." He let go of my arm and swung me around to face him. "Come, I'll race you to that old dead tree over there."

With that, he took off, running lightly through the meadow grass. Laughing, I swung on my heels to follow him. Colin was right. I was getting too morbid about the whole matter.

He waited for me beside the tree as I huffed toward him. Then he grabbed me in his arms and planted a quick kiss on my cheek.

"Remember how Paul and I kissed you when you got homesick for your folks because we couldn't bear to see you bawl? Well, the magic is back, Amy. There are more kisses where these came from—if you want them."

All I could remember was the time Paul kissed me here on the mine road when I cried because Kathryn refused to take me with her and her teenage friends to the carnival!

I laughed at the memory. "Colin, that was a long time ago. I must've been quite a brat in those days."

"You think that's all my kisses mean to you now, to heal your broken heart? Those days we could hardly stand to have you around. Now it's different. I could fall in love with you, if you'd let me."

"Please, Colin. You're a great guy, but I don't think you want to get serious about me, do you? Anyway, I don't."

Dropping his arms he gave his head a shake. "Well, I wanted you to know someone here still likes you."

"Thanks. That's sweet of you."

With a relieved grin he took my hand and we started back down the narrow road. Brandy and her kitten had already gone ahead, cavorting and springing on the weedy path.

Colin and I chatted and laughed as we strolled along, and I thought, How I needed this time away from the problems that confronted me in the old brick house. Was Colin right? Did I make too much of circumstantial evidence? And did I want more of his kisses? I knew he was trying to be nice to me, just clowning as usual, knowing I need it and taking advantage of it.

A few white clouds overhead were deepening to a dull gray in the southwest, the sunny afternoon swathed in mid-summer green. It was good to be alive.

When we reached the gate, Paul came to meet us, striding sure and full of purpose. He picked up Brandy in his arms and hugged her tightly. My heart beat faster. Did he have ominous news? Why had he come? And how could I ever have suspected him of mayhem?

"Good news!" he shouted as we came through the gate. "Dr. Blair was out again this afternoon and checked on Corrie-Mom. Her fever's down."

Brandy wriggled from her father's embrace. "Oh, I knew it would be. That's 'cause me and Amy prayed," she announced in a tone of voice that implied she was absolutely right.

I saw a quick light leap into Paul's eyes, as though this was something he had to give more thought.

13

I felt encouraged. Perhaps now that the fever was down, Aunt Corrie could make progress once more. And Brandy's acceptance of answered prayer thrilled me. I needed her backup assurance myself.

The next morning I was determined Mrs. Crosby had no further reason to shut me out of my great-aunt's room. I knocked on the door boldly this time.

"Well?"

The familiar gruff response made me smile. I wouldn't back down nor let the temerity of the nurse's tone of voice bother me.

"It's Amy. Please let me see my aunt today."

Some thirty seconds passed, and I raised my hand to knock again when she flung the door open.

"You can come in for a short second," she muttered as I shoved my way toward Aunt Corrie's bed. The face was white and drawn and she looked tired. Picking up one limp hand, I said,

"It's me, Aunt Corrie. How are you today?"

She lay with her eyes closed, not moving, and I wondered if she had slipped deeper into a stupor.

How my heart ached for her. She looked so pathetic, so pale and thin. Could she survive the awful fall? I stood silently beside the bed, pressing her hand as I mused.

The big dour nurse was beside me and pushed me rudely toward the door.

"You've saw her. Now you can go."

"Thanks for letting me in," I said, leaving reluctantly. I sighed as I went into my room. Why am I constantly shoved through doors? I thought, determined to resume my Bible reading to Aunt Corrie as soon as I could. Whether she could hear me or not, it wouldn't hurt her in any way.

Over Mrs. Crosby's protests I began our daily Scripture time the next day. Although Aunt Corrie's eyes seemed remote and dull, and it tore me apart to see her this way, I read verse upon verse. Now and then Brandy joined us, perched on a low stool, her green eyes soft as she listened.

"I guess her shut eyes can't see us," she said pensively one morning a few days later. "Do you think her ears can hear us?"

"Brandy, I couldn't say. But maybe she can hear, and we must let her listen, as God talks to her through his Word."

A week went by, with little or no change in Aunt Corrie's condition. I'd been so sure that once her fever was gone she would improve. I saw Colin and Kathryn only briefly, for as the Kansas summer lengthened, July days grew hot. Colin insisted nothing could drag him away from the air-conditioned comfort of his apartment. I knew Kathryn had a heavy schedule as reporter.

Paul had taken on extra work at the plant. He came home late, ate his dinner in silence, played briefly with Brandy, then went to his room on the lower floor at the rear end of the house. I was sure he was working too hard, but he refused to talk about it to me. Surely he was worried about Susan, too. He often drove to see her on weekends, and the two-hour drive in the heat exhausted him.

I occupied my time helping Annie Jane and playing with Brandy. Sometimes the little girl welcomed my friendly overtures; next time the hard, stony look was back in the green eyes and I kept out of her way. Now and then we swung on the old rope swing under the elms, but I sensed the child was restless and unhappy. I was thankful for Snow White, who seemed to take up much of her time.

The lazy days dragged with a heavy, humid somnolence that drained my energy. One afternoon I felt that if I didn't get out of Meriweather Hall I'd go mad. Slipping into white slacks and a pale sheer blue blouse, I jumped into my Honda and headed for town. Perhaps a few hours of browsing or shopping would perk up my spirits.

Stopping in the vast shopping center parking lot, I strolled from one brightly lit store to another. Women's colorful sunwear beckoned from large plate-glass windows. Armies of teddy bears stared out of a toy shop as I moved up and down the mall. I paused in front of a beauty shop and watched. Beauticians stroked and patted, sprayed and powdered, using a host of little pots and tubes, jars and brushes, on the plastic-draped women seated dreamily in beauty chairs.

With a sigh I moved on to the little ice-cream shop, mostly to get away from the searing summer heat. After ordering a vanilla malt, I slid into a booth, sipping the thick creamy concoction through a straw. I noticed a trim young woman at the cashier's counter, obviously paying for her purchases. She looked vaguely familiar. The finespun blond hair fell from a widow's peak on her forehead—where had I seen it before?

"Terri?" The words left my lips before I realized it. "Terri Baxter?"

The woman turned, then came toward my booth with a puzzled frown. "Yes? I'm Terri. Who—? Oh, I know. Amy Sutton, aren't you?" She scooted into the seat opposite me and reached for my hand, a smile etching her attractive face. "Wow, Amy, it's been a long time!"

Memories flooded back as I recalled the times we sat together in Sunday school at Aunt Corrie's church twelve years ago. I had not gone regularly since my return. Perhaps partly because I no longer remembered the people, and maybe because I felt needed at Meriweather Hall. Although I had been active in my church at home, here I didn't exactly fit in. I did take Brandy to Sunday school because I knew Aunt Corrie had begun the practice before her fall.

"Tell me about yourself," Terri said, once we had finished our greetings. "Are you living here, or just visiting?"

I shook my head. "I'm not sure. I came a few weeks after Aunt Corrie's fall, to do what I could to help. Mostly it's to make myself useful in whatever way possible. What about you?"

"I'm married to the most gorgeous hunk of man you ever saw," she lilted. "Craig Downing's very special, and we have two adorable kids. Barry's four and Londa will be two next month. I work at the hospital lab as a technician several shifts each week because we need the extra income."

"Don't we all," I said dryly. "Even the once-vast Meriweather wealth is almost nonexistent, they tell me."

"Bad investments? Your aunt was always a shrewd businesswoman, I thought."

"I don't know. All I know is that she's almost broke. At least, that's what Colin says."

"Would he have access to her funds? I'm not insinuating, you know, but—"

"I don't know that either. Aunt Corrie's lifelong friend Al McDivitt has the power of attorney, although I know nothing about him. I'm sure she trusts him."

"Al's reputation's tolerable, from what I hear," Terri added. "He surely wouldn't tamper. . . ."

"That's what bugs me. Who'd steal from a poor, defenseless woman? And why?"

Terri took a paper napkin and crumpled it into a small ball. "Today's world has taken leave of its senses. It seems there's no compassion any more."

"You're right," I said, pushing aside my malt. "The world is so cockeyed it has neither room nor time for the God we knew in Sunday school."

"Yes," Terri said, "that sums it up pretty well. Evil is taking its toll among so-called good people these days."

"It's too bad we get caught in the middle of it."

"So few people pay attention to God and his will, the meaning for life. Don't you think?"

"I'm sure you're right. People scoff. Where's his fairness when trouble comes? they say. Then when the Aunt Corries have accidents. . . ." I paused briefly. "Or get pushed," I added with a slight grimace.

"What do you mean, pushed?"

I shook my head. "If Brandy's to be believed. . . ."

"And she thinks. . . ?"

"At least that's what she says. Paul denies it, of course, and so does Colin. They think I'm flaky for even thinking it."

I wondered if I'd said too much. But I simply had to uncork my feelings. I knew I could trust Terri.

We parted shortly after promising each other we'd get together again. I drove home slowly, forgetting why I'd come to town. But the unexpected visit with my old friend perked me up and I was glad we had met.

Colin was lounging on the floral sofa in the cool, dim library when I got back. He sat up when I came in.

"Well, look who's here," he said, stretching himself languidly. "I thought maybe you'd forsaken us."

"I haven't seen you in more than a week," I said a trifle jadedly. "Maybe staring at all that money's made you myopic!"

He laughed boisterously. "I always knew you were too smart for us. But I've been . . . busy. Not that I wouldn't cross half the continent to be with you, my love."

"As you've proved this week," I mused dryly.

"Come now, Amy, you're not sore, are you? Did you miss me that much?"

With a sigh I sat down. "Colin, I'm in no mood for clowning today. What I'm concerned about is what's happening to Aunt Corrie's money. She used to be quite wealthy."

He leaned toward me and I noticed the nervous tap of his fingers on his knees. "Amy, so help me, all I know is that it's only a matter of time before she's broke."

I couldn't help wonder how much Colin knew. Moistening my lips, I replied, "I suppose you have no idea what's happening to it?"

"Not a speck," he said, shrugging his broad shoulders. "There must've been some bad investments."

"But who'd play around with her money without her knowledge?"

"Al McDivitt's the guy to ask. He's had power of attorney for a long time. But don't count on him sharing any information. None of us know the contents of her will. I'd say Al holds the answers."

I thought, Is it going to be up to me to dig out the facts? The idea sent shivers down my spine. One thing I didn't want to do was pry into Aunt Corrie's affairs. Yet someone had to do it.

I got to my feet and grinned at Colin. "Okay, if that's the way it's going to be, that's how it's going to be."

He looked rather startled at my response and jumped up from the sofa. I thought he seemed somewhat uneasy at my words, and it made me edgy. Even though I liked Colin, I mistrusted him a little. Why, I didn't know.

14

I wasted no time calling Al McDivitt's office and told him what I wanted. His voice sounded rather cocky, but I had never met him and decided not to jump to conclusions.

"If you come to my office, I'll discuss this with you in person," he said affably. "But there's really not much I can tell you."

"I'll be there in half an hour," I promised.

I wanted to see him before dinner and had no time to lose. In minutes I was in my car, weaving through late-afternoon traffic toward town. The day ran slowly, heavy like honey, sweet and golden. Already the sun slanted toward the west and shreds of cloud caught fire, one after another, from the afterglow.

Minutes later I pulled up before the towering gray stone office building where Aunt Corrie's legal adviser rented a suite of rooms.

When I entered the first room his receptionist looked up from her typewriter, and I told her of our phone conversation.

"Mr. McDivitt will see you shortly," she said crisply, pointing to a chair, and resumed her typing.

I sat down to wait, glancing around the large airy well-lighted room. The walls were painted a pale mauve, blending with the figured drapes that were pulled back from spacious windows. Plants grew luxuriant from wicker-potted stands. An opulent graciousness seemed to pervade the suite.

A few minutes later the phone buzzed. The receptionist spoke a few words, then turned to me. "Mr. McDivitt will see you now."

I walked into his large office, done in mahogany and pale yellow. The man who got up from behind the huge desk was stocky and short, with a thick crop of grayish-brown hair tumbling from his forehead. He was dressed in a light green leisure suit and creamy white shirt with open collar. The wide planes of his face were clean-shaven, and his eyes behind wire-rimmed spectacles a pale amber. He reached out his hand.

"You're Miss Sutton?" he asked, his voice rather low and husky.

"Yes. As I told you on the phone I came to be with my great-aunt Corinda Ward as soon as I heard she needed me."

He pulled out a soft green chair for me, then returned behind his desk and folded his hands in front of him.

"What exactly do you want of me?"

I drew a deep breath. "Mr. McDivitt, I understand you have power of attorney over Aunt Corrie's affairs. I'm deeply concerned, for obviously her money is disappearing at an alarming rate. Surely you're aware of what's going on?"

He leaned back in his chair and shook his head slowly. "Certainly you can't expect me to divulge any information which I hold in strictest confidence to my client! Not only is it unethical, I gave Corinda Ward my word—"

"But she's helpless!" I blurted out. "As her niece I have

a right to know what is going on, since she is obviously unaware of anything."

"What makes you think you have this right?" he asked, his gaze narrowing.

"I'm her only living blood relative. And if what I suspect is true, someone's trying to get her out of the way. If this is so—"

"You don't know what you're saying!" he cut in, and I thought he sounded quite disturbed. "You surely aren't accusing me of something as serious as what I think you mean, are you?"

"I. . . ." For a moment his bluntness stymied me. Then I plunged on. "I wondered who her heirs are. Whoever stands to inherit might have a reason to want her out of the way."

"And you think I'd tell you?" His voice sounded incredulous. "You'd actually expect me to betray my client's confidence?"

"In other words, you're saying you won't tell me anything? That you're not concerned?" I shot back with a burst of confidence.

He removed his glasses and laid them on his desk, then faced me squarely. "I'm far more concerned than you know, Miss Sutton. If her funds are vanishing, I'd surely do all I could to halt it, wouldn't I?"

"I would think so," I said, a trifle deflated. "But if I had some answers—"

"I can't tell you more than that, Miss Sutton." He replaced his glasses and got to his feet. I knew he was dismissing me, and I thanked him politely for his time and left.

Gray clouds had pulled over the horizon as I walked to

my car. The whole thing puzzled me. I couldn't prove it, but I was almost certain Al McDivitt was covering up something, and the sooner I found out what it was, the better.

I was caught in the snarl of five-o'clock traffic, and it was nearly six when I steered my Honda into Meriweather Hall's graveled drive.

As I hurried into the house, Paul came from his room, smelling of after-shave lotion, dressed for dinner.

"Looks like I beat you this time, Amy," he said with a wry smile. "The warm afternoon hasn't wilted you the way it's zonked me."

"I feel as if I've been squeezed through the wringer. Paul, I'm just furious!" I burst out.

"Why? What's bugging you now?"

I walked up to him and laid a hand on his shoulder. "We've got to stop whoever's siphoning off Aunt Corrie's money! I just came from Al McDivitt's office."

"Amy! You didn't. You surely don't suspect—"

"I'm not sure what I think. But I'll wager the guy knows more than he's telling."

"Al has been a longtime family friend, Amy. If you think for one second Corrie-Mom didn't trust him to handle her money, you're mistaken. Why not bug off?"

I jerked my hand away. What ailed Paul Ward? Couldn't he see something was horribly wrong? Yet why should he hold me off? No, I wasn't ready to "bug off," as he had said. The riddle must be solved, and I realized again it was up to me. I doubted that Colin would be of help, although I planned to talk to him.

We ate dinner in almost total silence. Paul spoke only briefly, mostly addressing Brandy, who bubbled with chatter.

"Snow White's a super kitten," she babbled. "Absolutely tremendous."

"Yes? What's she done that so special?" Paul asked.

"She chases all over the place and hides from me and then I hide from her. We play hide-and-seek. I'm usually *it*, because I gotta find her!" She laughed heartily.

As Annie Jane brought in the coconut pie, Paul said, "Be sure Brandy's ready to leave in the morning. We want to get as early a start as possible."

I jerked up my head. "Leave? Where are you taking Brandy?" I burst out a trifle irritably.

"I'm going to visit Sue and I want to take our daughter with me," he said a bit coldly.

For the past several weekends Paul had visited his sick wife at the clinic. Yet he seldom took Brandy, since it seemed to upset the child to see her mother bedridden.

"But—but you know how. . . ," I began, then paused, glancing at Brandy. The happy smiles had faded and the stony look was back in her green eyes. No doubt, Brandy was in for another sharp blow.

"Brandy wants to see her mother," Paul said blandly. "Don't you, Brandy?"

The little girl turned away quickly, then jumped from her chair. "Oh, my poor momma!" she cried, and fled from the room.

I stared at Paul. Usually he was quiet and gentle. Why was he being cruel now? He flinched under my scrutiny, got up abruptly, and left the table.

I finished my piece of pie and cleared the dishes from the table. Needing to do something to occupy my roiling thoughts, I tied one of Annie Jane's big aprons around my waist. Over her mild protests, I washed the dishes. My thoughts milled as I sudsed, scrubbed, and rinsed the delicate china.

Tomorrow was Saturday. I knew I'd miss Brandy since we had often made a game of cleaning her room and washing and fixing her hair. Yes, of course she needed to see her "poor momma," for surely Susan must want to see her child, too. What was the matter with me? Just because Brandy had finally begun to respond to my love and care was no sign I had any hold over her. Yet, she had steered away from her black moods and I was afraid she would retreat if she faced another traumatic scene after seeing her sick mother. I wanted to protect her, shield her from more hurt I was sure she would encounter.

After finishing the dishes, I hurried upstairs to my room, thankful that I didn't see either Paul or Brandy. I wouldn't have known how to face them just now. I read a while, penned a brief letter to Eric, and went to bed.

When I awoke the next morning Paul and Brandy had gone. The house seemed ominously quiet and strangely empty. I heard only the soft sounds of Mrs. Crosby's ministrations from Aunt Corrie's bedroom and an occasional slam of a door downstairs.

After the mail came, I went into the library to read the two letters the mailman had left for me. One was from Eric, the other from Shannon Greer, one of my teacher-friends at Peter Conrad. I read Shannon's first.

"You are crazy for copping out on that cruise!" she scolded me mildly. "Whatever your reasons—and I guess I'll never quite understand them unless you've finally made up your mind about Eric—I'll see you back in your classroom in another three weeks."

Three weeks! Time was running out for me. I was scheduled to be back in my fifth-grade classroom in less than a month and my problems here at Meriweather Hall were far from resolution.

Should I cancel my contract with the school and stay here? The idea haunted me when I thought about it. Dear Lord, what shall I do?

Idly I picked up the letter from Eric. It was dated the first of August. I tore open the flap and hastily scanned the brief lines. The gist of the letter sprang at me in a few hurried sentences, "Since I'm going to the church conference and Waylan isn't much out of my way, Amy, I thought I'd stop by for a day or so to see you . . . arriving some time Saturday afternoon. I hope it's okay. . . ."

Eric! Coming to Meriweather Hall? *Today?* I didn't know whether I wanted to see him or not. I had been too occupied with problems here lately to give much thought to my own feelings toward him.

As I replaced the letter in the envelope I heard the front door slam and footsteps in the hall. Through the open library door I caught a glimpse of Colin. He looked as debonair and lovable as ever. *When* would I ever stop feeling giddy and spirited when Colin Ward came near me?

"Hi!" he called out when he spied me in the library. "How's my one-and-only, my joy, my delight?" He stooped down and kissed the top of my head.

I waved him into a chair. "In a dither or quandary, whatever," I parried. "In a dither because I'm trying to solve the mystery of Aunt Corrie's disappearing money, and in a quandary because Eric Stone is stopping by for a visit. He's arriving today."

Colin pretended agony. "Oh, no! And I've had no luck persuading you to come away with me. Amy, darling, don't

117

tell me you're going to pack up and ride into the western sunset with your preacher."

"I'm not sure what I want," I said rather helplessly. "If I only knew. But with my trying to track down the puzzles surrounding Meriweather Hall—"

"Are you onto something, Amy?" he cut in, a sudden wary look in his eyes.

"Look, Colin, I'm concerned that my aunt won't be destitute, so I went to see Al McDivitt yesterday."

"And what did Al tell you?"

"Exactly nothing. But I'm convinced something's going on that I should know. And so help me, I'm going to find out what it is!"

Colin looked away, then turned back to me. "Look Amy, I want to see this problem solved as much as you do, but if you tangle with Al McDivitt, you could be sorry. The guy knows what he's doing, believe me."

"If he does, why is he so secretive about it?" I demanded. "I aim to see a lawyer next week, someone who will make him reveal what he knows."

Did I imagine it, or did Colin's face blanch for a moment? Whatever was rotten here, I knew I must stay and find out what it was.

15

I was almost sorry Paul and Brandy were away. Some-how I needed their backup support for Eric's visit, although for the life of me I didn't know what either of them could do. Still, I had work to do and went first of all into the kitchen to inform Annie Jane. She was bending over a big pan of whole wheat bread dough.

"A friend is dropping by for a few days," I told her. "He's on his way back from a church conference and wants to see me."

She lifted her floury hands and placed them on her hips. "I s'pose he'll expect to be treated like company," she muttered.

"Oh, no! Eric's really common. He'll fit in nicely. Don't let him worry you a bit."

"Well," she paused to whack her dough a time or two, "I'd figured with Mr. Paul and the little miss gone, we'd sort of help ourselves. This throws a monkey wrench—"

"No, no," I protested."I'll help you. And please treat Eric as you treat me. After all, he's trying to persuade me to marry him," I added whimsically.

"I sure hope he does," she said as she thumped the dough soundly and gave me a mock glower. "But don't worry. I'll fix grub that's fittin'."

With a short laugh I retraced my steps to the library.

Colin had gone. I plumped the pillows on the sofa and straightened the faded photo on the mantel. The house seemed ominous and quiet. I missed Brandy's patter through the house, her squeals of laughter as she chased her pet kitten from room to room. I remembered my promise to feed Snow White and the rest of Thomasina's brood and made a mental note to carry a pan of milk to the barn.

I wondered if Paul and Brandy had arrived at the clinic, for I knew it was a wearying two-hour drive. Fortunately, Paul had found a place for Susan where rates were not unreasonably steep. How would Brandy respond to her mother? And would Susan offer her exuberant little daughter the attention she desperately craved? I would ask Paul about it later. What was important to Brandy was suddenly important to me.

I ate an egg-and-chicken sandwich for lunch, garnished with a slice of tomato, and checked the large airy rooms in the old brick house once more. Everything was spotless in spite of its genteel shabbiness.

At four I showered and slipped into a sleeveless dress of Caribbean blue, banded at the neckline and waist with brown. I brushed my hair, fastened tiny sapphire earrings onto my ears, and went down to the library to wait for Eric's arrival.

The ticking of the hall clock sounded unusually loud, and the emptiness of the old mansion almost shouted at me. I closed the shutters and turned on the fan. Its constant hum seemed to erase some of the dead silence.

With a sigh I sat down on the sofa and let my thoughts wander. Now that Eric was coming I knew I must give him an answer. He was good and kind, gentle, handsome, and all a girl could wish for in a husband. I knew I was silly for not falling head-over-heels in love with him, and I couldn't understand it. Perhaps seeing him again would stir up my feelings so I could decide. I fervently hoped so.

At the sound of a car in the drive I jumped up, patted my hair hurriedly, and went toward the front door.

I opened it before the bell rang.

"Eric! Do come in," I cried, pulling him inside. He stepped into the hall, tall and tanned, his tawny hair tousled from the wind.

Taking my hands in his, he smiled, his blue eyes twinkling. "Amy. . . . You look marvelous! You've no idea how I've missed you."

I lifted my face for his light kiss and took his arm. "Let's go into the library. We've a lot of news to catch up on, don't we? Tell me about the conference."

"After you," he said, stepping back and following me into the dim, quiet library. I positioned the fan so that the cool air circulated over us as we sat down together on the sofa.

The silence between us was rather awkward. If only Brandy and Paul were here, I'd feel more at ease, I thought again, relaxing my clenched fingers.

Eric leaned toward me. "Tell me about yourself first, Amy. Are you accomplishing here what you'd hoped?"

"Oh, Eric, I don't know. There are still so many puzzles. . . ." I found myself pouring out the mysteries that enshrouded the old mansion and which seemed so hard to unravel.

"I guess I feel especially alone today, with both Paul and Brandy gone," I finished lamely.

"But that gives us a better chance to talk, to clear the air between us," he suggested.

121

I tensed uneasily. "Yes, I guess so. Tell me, how are things with you, Eric? The church, and your people?"

He crossed his legs and laced his fingers across his knees. "The conference was great. I've been offered a large church in Philadelphia," he said. "It's located in a suburban area in the midst of a whole new subdivision. Think of the potential mission, Amy! I'm really excited about it. What do you think of the prospect?"

"I think it's terrific. Oh, Eric, it's fabulous," I gushed. "You'll be the right preacher there, and you'll do just great. When do you move?"

"Well, there's one stipulation." He paused and eyed me with a twinkle. "They don't want a single pastor. Of course, I told them I had the perfect, most beautiful woman all picked out to take care of the problem. So it's up to you, my dearest Amy."

The love and longing that crept into his blue eyes touched me, and I yearned to throw my arms around him and promise to marry him as soon as possible. Yet something held me back.

I lowered my gaze, then lifted my face. "Eric, I don't know. I have . . . such a time deciding."

A hurt look flickered over his face, then was gone. "Well," he said, a faint smile touching his lips, "you've had gigantic problems on your mind. No wonder you haven't had time to think. Maybe by Monday when I leave, I'll have my answer."

At that moment I saw Annie Jane beckoning me at the door, and I knew dinner was ready. With a relieved sigh I got up.

"Come," I told Eric, "Annie Jane says dinner is ready. Let's see what she's fixed for us."

The broiled perch fillets, tossed green salad, and fresh-baked whole-wheat bread were tasty. Eric and I grew relaxed as we ate.

He pushed himself away from the table and folded his napkin neatly after he had finished his triangle of apple pie.

"Amy, I needn't tell you how I like home cooking! Think you could qualify as a cook?"

I laughed lightly, knowing he liked to tease. Then I cupped my chin in my hands, propped my elbows on the table, and faced him.

"Annie Jane's had more experience, but I think I could match her. If you don't believe me, ask Paul."

"Paul? Oh, your Aunt Corrie's stepson. Yes, of course." He fell silent.

As I made a move to get up, Eric was behind me and pulled away my chair. Had I been tactless to mention Paul? I hadn't done it purposely.

"You haven't met Aunt Corrie. Why don't we go upstairs and see her? She won't know you, naturally, but I'd like you to see her," I said, groping for time.

He followed me up the stairs and into my aunt's room. Nurse Crosby stood aside with her usual scowl after she admitted us.

Aunt Corrie's face was so white and still I feared she was ill, but I saw the steady rise and fall of her chest under the sheet.

"Aunt Corrie," I said, moving near the bed, "we have a guest. Eric Stone has stopped by for a little visit on his way home from church conference. I—I think you'll like Eric."

He stood beside me and reached out a gentle hand to touch her forehead. "Amy's told me all about you," he said.

"The Lord's with you, whether you realize it or not. He's promised never to leave nor forsake his own."

She made no move to indicate she had heard. I thought, How long will she be shut away in the prison of her own body, never making contact?

Suddenly I was aware that Eric had begun to pray, his words rippling like soft rain in the quiet room. *Why can't I love this beautiful man?* I cried in my heart. He had so much to give, to share.

As we left the room a few minutes later my heart was heavy. What if I married Eric? Love would surely come, I assured myself. He could take this large church in Philadelphia, I would be cherished by the women's missionary societies, and we'd share our love and service in the community together. But something held me back.

The next morning Eric and I went to church together. He mingled with people as though it was the most natural thing in the world. I couldn't understand why God didn't *make* me love him.

Although the service was moving and reverent yet lively, my thoughts were not on the message. They boiled and tumbled in my mind and I stirred restlessly. Perhaps if I left all this mystery, these problems behind, I could more fully concentrate on loving this gentle, dynamic, divinely anointed man.

Eric had conspired with Annie Jane to take me downtown to a quiet little restaurant for lunch. He was so full of dreams, his work of the future in God's kingdom, that I simply reveled in the tender atmosphere that seemed to encircle us in the dark mahogany booth. The grilled steaks, when the waitress brought them, were delicious.

The August afternoon had grown warm and sultry, and I

wished Paul and Brandy could be spared the drive on the scorching asphalt highways.

When we reached the Meriweather Hall, I glanced at the carriage-house garage. Paul's car wasn't there.

"I guess they're not back yet," I said.

"Who? Oh, you mean Paul and his daughter."

"Brandy's quite a pill on the road, especially when it's so hot, Paul says."

Eric didn't answer. We walked into the house together and went back into the library. I pulled the drapes against the heat and turned on the fan. The room still seemed warm.

Avoiding Eric's eyes, I began to chatter about anything that popped into my head: Brandy's pet kitten, the walk to the nearby mine, Aunt Corrie's vegetable garden. . . .

Abruptly Eric laid a hand on my arm. "You needn't think up excuses not to talk about what you know we must discuss. Obviously you're not ready to give me your answer." The hurt look was back in his eyes.

"I'm sorry, Eric. It's just that—"

The familiar sound of Paul's blue sedan in the drive interrupted my words and I glanced toward the doorway. Minutes later I heard the front door slam and Brandy's eager voice in the hall.

I jumped to my feet when she stepped into the doorway of the library and hurried toward her.

"Brandy, you okay?"

She held me away for a minute, and I saw her green eyes glisten with tears. Then she rushed into my arms and began to cry.

"Oh, Amy . . . Amy. . . ." Great gulping sobs wrenched her shoulders and I held her close, patting her gently.

"Brandy—Brandy, I'm here with you!" It was all I could think to say.

I heard Paul's footsteps behind me and my gaze flew to his tortured face. All I saw was suffering love. He must've seen Eric, for I noticed the questioning look in his dark eyes.

With a start I remembered my manners. "Paul—Brandy, this is Eric Stone, my—my friend from California. He—he stopped by on his way back from conference in Indiana. It—it was a surprise," I fumbled awkwardly with my words.

Paul and Eric exchanged pleasantries while I told Brandy about Snow White.

"I gave her plenty of milk, and she followed me around because she missed you so much," I said.

"Then at least, she's okay."

"Yes. How is Susan?" I asked, turning to Paul after I could trust myself to speak calmly.

"She—she's developed a bronchial condition and she's very weak. It's hard to say."

"Oh, Paul, I'm so sorry!"

Paul stood awkwardly in the center of the room. Then he turned to Brandy. "Come, Brandy," he said abruptly. "You'd better go upstairs to your room now."

She glanced sideways at me and I nodded. Without a word she left the room with her father. I came back and sat down on the sofa again.

Eric stared at the empty doorway, then looked at me. I noticed the obvious sorrow in his eyes, for Susan's condition, I supposed, or because of my evasiveness.

With a troubled sigh he rose to his feet. "Well, I guess I'd better be on my way, Amy. It's a long drive to California."

"Now, Eric? But I thought you were going to wait until morning."

He looked at me tenderly and shook his head. "No, Amy. I came for my answer and I got it. Now I must leave."

"But I haven't said—"

"You didn't have to, my dearest," he said, his voice low and sad. "I saw your eyes light up the minute Paul Ward walked into the house. I know now that you love that man, the kind of love I'd hoped you'd offer me."

I felt myself grow limp with disbelief. "But you're wrong, Eric!" I cried. "I *can't* love Paul. He's married . . . and his wife—oh, Eric. It's wrong for me to love a married man. Don't you see? If you want me, I—I—I'll marry you. I know I can make you happy. We—we'll serve that church in Philadelphia together!" I flew up to him and threw my arms around his neck.

He pushed me away firmly. "No, Amy. You don't love me. Face it. You and I can never be happy as long as your feelings toward me are secondhand. You know that as well as I do."

I drew back as though he had slapped me. Was Eric right? How could he have seen what I didn't recognize in myself?

With a brave smile and a wave of his hand he swung around and left the room without turning back. I stood there, unable to move.

When I heard the door slam behind him, I knew Eric Stone was out of my life forever. And I didn't know whether to be glad or sad.

16

The next day I awoke to a quiet, cool August morning. Sumac against the stone walls to the west flaunted scarlet tips. The cloudless dawn was a turquoise sea where it shaded from faint emerald through jade to indigo, then to purple where it met and fused with the sky.

I thought of Eric, somber and hurting on his lonely drive back to California, and I shook my head fiercely. I'd wanted so much to love him, to share his life, and it made me angry with myself because I couldn't care enough.

His accusing words still rang in my ears, daring to tell me I loved Paul Ward, and I sighed deeply. I had always adored Paul as long as I'd known him. But love? Had Eric read something in my eyes, my soul, that I didn't even know existed? Well, it wasn't true. Because Paul was married I had steeled myself against any deep feelings toward him. Besides, his faith was almost nonexistent. It would never work. I firmly pushed the thought from my mind.

With a square jut to my jaw I got up and dressed, determined to put Paul completely out of my mind. My agenda was full today and I knew I must get to work.

Brandy waited for me at the breakfast table. "Listen to my cereal," she called out when I sat down with my bowl of cooked oatmeal. "It goes 'snap, popple, crack.' Why does it talk like that?"

128

I smiled indulgently. "Oh, I guess it's lonesome and knows you're lonesome so the two of you can talk and crunch together!"

"I'm *not* lonesome!" she burst out vehemently. "My momma told me yesterday I can never be lonesome 'cause Jesus is with me."

"And she's right," I told her. "Oh, we may get lost in a deep blue fog sometimes, but if we follow closely he will lead us out."

She was silent for a moment, then eyed me quizzically. "Is that what your Eric preacher told you? And is it true that you're going to marry him and leave me?"

"No, I'm not going to marry Eric. Whatever gave you that idea?"

"My daddy said that would be the very bestest thing for you, although I can't see why. If you'd go away I'd be alone here when Daddy's at work—"

"But I'm not leaving yet, no matter what your father says," I said in a fierce voice. Maybe Paul had changed his mind about wanting me here, but I wasn't finished with my job. I'd stay as long as I was needed, and until I was convinced it was over.

Brandy finished her cereal, carried her bowl and spoon to the sink, and slammed out of the house.

After I had eaten my oatmeal and toast I went upstairs to get my Bible for my time alone with Aunt Corrie.

"Don't keep her long," Mrs. Crosby grumped when I came into the room. "She don't seem as restful as usual."

I assured Crosby I wouldn't tire her, and sat down at the bedside. "Aunt Corrie," I said before opening my Bible, "I don't know if I did the right thing, but I sent one young man away from here yesterday with a broken heart and it disturbs me. Still, when a person doesn't love—isn't in love with him, what else can one do?"

She lay with her eyes closed. Mrs. Crosby had mentioned she was restless, but I thought she was very quiet.

I opened my Bible and began to read from Psalm 27: " 'Wait on the Lord: be of good courage, and he shall strengthen thine heart.' Believe it, Aunt Corrie. He'll give you the strength you need, and me the strength I need too."

Suddenly the half-lidded eyes flew open and I saw recognition in them, an awareness of things going on around her.

"Aunt Corrie!" I cried. "You *know* I'm here, don't you? You can see me. Oh, please don't go away. Please stay!"

Her clear gaze held mine for a few seconds, then slowly clouded over. For a few brief moments Aunt Corrie had caught a glimpse outside of her prison wall; but the shadow had fallen over her spirit again.

My step was lighter as I left the room. Aunt Corrie had shown a rational side of her being today. This was proof that it was possible for her to recover in time. If only she would come out of her stupor, we'd know if she was really pushed, or what had happened on the stairs that day.

I wanted to share the good news with someone, but I wasn't sure with whom. I decided to tell neither Paul nor Colin, for they'd seemed upset when I'd mentioned it previously. I needed more time before I told them.

Just then I heard Kathryn's short, clicking footsteps down the hall. She was undoubtedly bringing more medication.

When she came out of Aunt Corrie's room some time later, I waited for her in the hall. As usual, she looked cool and relaxed in her ice-blue dress with a froth of ruffle around the neckline. Her face lit into a quick smile when she saw me.

"Amy! Don't tell me you have good news," she said in her quick, breathless way.

"How'd you guess?"

"It's written all over you. So you're going to marry Eric Stone? Colin told me yesterday that he was here to see you."

I felt a flush dye my face. Colin had jumped to conclusions again. "Wrong. I told Eric I didn't love him, and he left late yesterday afternoon."

"But why? You'd have made a perfect pair," she said, a disappointed look in her eyes. "I want you to be happy, Amy. What could be better for you?"

"I appreciate your concern, Kathryn, but I can't marry someone I don't love, even for all the seemingly right reasons," I said quietly. "My good news is that Aunt Corrie opened her eyes again today. The gaze was as clear and lucid as mine and yours are right now."

"Did she say anything?"

I shook my head. "No, but one of these times she will. You can be sure of that."

"That would be great," she said, but I thought she didn't sound overly enthusiastic. She had looked tired lately and I could understand her lack of enthusiasm.

With a quick smile she whirled around. "Sorry. I gotta run. I'm due to do an interview at eleven."

I heard the hurried clicking of her heels along the hall and down the stairs until she slammed out of the house.

Brandy barreled out of her room, her green eyes tough and hard. "You told *her* and not *me!*" she pouted. "Why didn't you tell me about Grandma Corrie? I thought you were my friend. Well, you're not!"

"Oh, Brandy," I said with a deep sigh. "I wanted to tell you but you went out after breakfast to play with Snow White. I didn't hear you come back into the house. I just had to share the good news with someone, and your Aunt Kathryn was here. I *am* your friend, please believe me."

The bitter glints in her green eyes wavered and she stared at me. "Really?"

"Of course, dear."

In a flash the storm was over, and Brandy rushed toward me with open arms. "Oh, Amy, please don't ever leave me, like Momma!"

A sob caught in my throat. How could I tell this child that I couldn't remain forever? That I would have to leave eventually?

"I'll not leave for a long time," I said. "And that's a promise."

That did it. I had to call the school principal and tell him that I was resigning. Things were beginning to move here now and I had to stay until they were settled. I couldn't leave now if I wanted to.

For the past several weeks I had seen Brandy soften, not only toward me but as an individual. The hurt she had suffered was beginning to heal. And that was one more reason I had to stay. She needed me more than ever, especially now that her mother lay dying.

After lunch I called Daryl Swanson, a lawyer I had decided might help me. He agreed to see me at three.

I liked Mr. Swanson immediately. His cropped white hair and benign smile inspired confidence, and when I found myself sitting in his simply furnished office, I quickly poured out my story. He listened intently, and I'm sure he was mentally taking notes.

"Then you don't know who your great-aunt's heirs are?" he asked pointedly after I had finished my story.

"No. Al McDivitt refuses to give me that information."

"I see you have a problem there," he said, tapping a pen on his desk. "If what you say about her money dwindling is true, we can, through a court order, make him tell what he knows. I also feel that another needed step is to take the legal power away from McDivitt and appoint you as your great-aunt's guardian."

"Me!" the word exploded from my lips. "But I don't see—"

"As her only living blood relative, you can be given that right. McDivitt will be requested by Kansas law to give an accounting of his duties and his use—or misuse—of your great-aunt's funds. This accounting would be due in thirty days. After that, the bank can take over as conservator."

I caught my breath sharply. Would this move involve Colin in any way? Would he then have actual access. . . ? And if I were listed as an heir, would the three stepchildren become even more antagonistic, maybe even hostile toward me? My problems would probably mushroom, but I had to do what was best for Aunt Corinda.

"I trust this is a satisfactory way of solving matters for you, Miss Sutton," Mr. Swanson said, getting to his feet. "This is the one way of getting matters out of McDivitt's hands. And that's the important step right now."

Nodding my thanks, I left the office and hurried home. I didn't like the idea of being appointed Aunt Corrie's guardian, but under the circumstances there wasn't much else I could do. We still had thirty days for McDivitt to act.

"Lord," I prayed, "let me have a breakthrough before then!"

As I came into the house I heard sharp words and screams from upstairs and hurried to find out what was going on. The crusty nurse stood in front of Brandy, a sullen look on her face.

"You done it and you'd better apologize right now!" she stormed.

Brandy's green eyes were steely. "Try and make me. You just try!" She placed her hands on her hips and stuck out her tongue.

"Brandy!" I ordered. "What's going on?"

She defied me with an angry look. "None of your business, Amy. It's between me 'n her." She pointed an accusing finger at Mrs. Crosby.

"What's the matter, Mrs. Crosby?" I asked, trying to maintain a level tone of voice.

"Now you're taking *her* side!" Brandy lashed out at me. "You're not my friend, like you said. But serves her right. She had it coming to her."

"Had what coming? Will someone please tell me what's going on?" I demanded.

Mrs. Crosby turned to me with an exaggerated sigh. "This young lady put snails in my cot, that's what!"

I stifled the impulse to laugh. Obviously it was Brandy's way of getting even with the crabby old nurse for something.

Turning to Brandy, I said, "Is this true?"

Her eyes glittered and her fingers clenched into fists. She was obviously upset about it.

"Is this true, Brandy?" I repeated in a firm tone.

"Yes." She nodded vigorously. "I snuck in her room when she was carrying out the dirty sheets."

"But why?"

Brandy glared at Mrs. Crosby until the older woman turned away. " 'Cause she chased Snow White out of Grandma Corrie's room, that's why. All I wanted was to show Grandma Corrie my pet. You said she was waking up and I was sure she'd be pleased. Then this witchy old lady—"

"Brandy!" I cut in sharply. "I'll have no more talk like that."

"She had no truck bringin' a beast into the sickroom!" fumed the burly nurse.

"Snow White's no beast. She's a tiny little pussycat. And then Mrs. Crosby takes a flyswatter and chases poor Snow White all the way downstairs. Poor Snow White hiked under the sofa in the library. Now she's scared to come out. And it's her fault!"

I placed a placating hand on Mrs. Crosby's shoulder. "Brandy's obviously very upset, and I hope you can forgive her childish antics," I said. "It wasn't nice, and I'll deal with her about the snails. Brandy and I will come in later and clean up the mess."

Without a word the old nurse swung around and lumbered back into Aunt Corrie's room with a slam of the door.

I took Brandy's arm, led her to my room, and motioned her to sit down. She had grown quiet, which was unusual for the exuberant little girl.

Now she gazed at me with wistful eyes. "I s'pose you'll turn me into a frog or something horribly wicked for what I did," she pouted.

"No, I shan't," I told her. "I just wanted to tell you that what you did wasn't nice—but you know that already. There are better ways of dealing with our problems than by plotting revenge."

135

"What kind of ways?"

"Forgiveness is God's way, you know. Forgiveness and love."

"But I can't forget her chasing Snow White, and Snow White won't forgive being chased either! Nobody loves Mrs. Crosby. Not even you!"

I smiled quietly at the child's perception. I hoped she had gotten it all out of her system. Her stormy look subsided.

"Now that's over, why not coax Snow White out and forget it happened?" I said finally.

Without a word she scrambled to her feet and flew out of the room. She was probably glad her *session* with me was over. I supposed she would cajole her kitten out from under the sofa in one way or another. With a sigh I went to Aunt Corrie's room and scooped up the snails from Mrs. Crosby's cot, tossed them into the wastebasket, and changed the sheets.

Aunt Corrie seemed to be sleeping peacefully, and I paused only long enough to pat her soft white cheek.

Going downstairs to the hall phone, I made a phone call to Peter Conrad's principal and tendered my resignation. He was surprised but understanding.

"Under the circumstances I see your first duty is toward your family," he said. "Please send us the notice of your resignation in writing by mail, Amy, and we'll handle it at this end. And any time you need references, let me know. You are an excellent teacher."

I knew I'd miss Shannon and Faye and the other teachers who had become my friends as well as co-workers. But there was no way I could leave Meriweather Hall now.

The rest of the day passed swiftly. After dinner and be-

136

fore twilight set in, I brought in a big panful of ripe tomatoes and crisp green cucumbers from the vegetable garden. The heat still hung over the land and I felt like a wilted lettuce leaf.

Brandy followed me into the house and watched as I rinsed the vegetables in the sink and placed them in the crisper of the refrigerator.

"Now I guess you'll make me eat more veggies," she grimaced as I turned to face her.

"You're absolutely right, Brandy. Some day when you have a strong healthy body you'll thank me."

She eyed me petulantly. "How about swinging me on the old rope swing? You haven't done it in a long time."

"You're absolutely right again. Let's go."

For some time I pushed the swing back and forth. The sun had slipped below the horizon and the red glow at the rim of the world faded into pink. The sky turned from pale mauve to purple, and the unearthly stillness of a Kansas twilight crept stealthily over the land. Its peacefulness stole over me and I felt suddenly content.

The swing moved slower and slower and finally it stopped. Brandy turned her head and grinned impishly.

"I bet you liked it when my daddy pushed you on the swing, didn't you?"

"Wha—? Oh, yes." I recalled having told Brandy about the times Paul had pushed the swing, just as I was doing now. "Yes, it made me happy. Your daddy was just seventeen then. I'm sure he's forgotten all about it."

"I don't think so. Don't you wish he'd swing you again?"

My heart gave a lurch, but I laughed lightly. "Oh, I don't know. I'm big and grown up now."

"I hope you'll always be around to swing me, Amy," she answered simply.

137

There it was again. *Always* was a big word, a forever word. How would I deal with Brandy when my business here was settled and I returned to California? If Aunt Corrie continued to improve, I could be ready to leave by early winter. When I strolled into the house later, I tried to push aside the thought of leaving Meriweather Hall, for I felt as though I belonged here. But I knew I didn't.

The next morning when I went in to read to Aunt Corrie she seemed far away and remote, the dull, glazed look back in her eyes. My heart sank. I was so sure she was making progress. Now she was back in a stupor again.

I was alone in the room with my great-aunt, for I had persuaded Mrs. Crosby to go into the kitchen for a cup of tea. I let the tears course down my cheeks. Why had my hopes for Aunt Corrie's recovery been dashed again?

"Dear Lord," I prayed fervently, "what's the answer? I had so hoped. . . ."

Suddenly I spotted the large bottle of brown liquid medication on the bedside stand, still almost full since Kathryn's delivery yesterday. I picked it up and opened the cap, holding it under my nose for a whiff.

The doctor had assured me there was nothing in the medication that would drug Aunt Corrie. Yet the thought of sedation tantalized my mind. Could the nearly full bottle contain an added ingredient, something someone might have slipped into it?

A wild idea hit me, and I hurried to my room for an empty aspirin bottle. I stopped in the bathroom, rinsed it, and rushed back into Aunt Corrie's bedroom. Tilting the full bottle, I carefully poured a bit of the liquid into the aspirin bottle and screwed the cap back on. My hands shook, for what I was about to do was a secret I would share with no one in this house just yet.

I heard Mrs. Crosby's heavy footsteps clomping up the stairs and hurriedly wiped the large bottle, almost dropping it in the process.

Slipping the aspirin bottle under my armpit, I picked up my Bible and resumed my place beside the bed.

Just then the hefty nurse came into the room, her rugged face creased into its usual frown.

"Time to go," she announced crisply.

I glanced up and nodded. "Yes, of course. I hope you enjoyed your cup of tea with Annie Jane."

She grunted a little and I went out of the room, clutching the small bottle with its sample of medication in my hand. This afternoon I would take it to Terri and ask her to test the contents in her lab.

17

Tucking the aspirin bottle with Aunt Corrie's medication into my purse, I dressed to go out. I didn't tell anyone where I was going, but as I headed for the front hall Brandy waylaid me.

"Where are you going, Amy?" she asked, probably out of habit.

"I'm taking a quick trip to town, dear," I said rather absently because I was in a hurry.

"Can I go with you?"

"I'm sorry, Brandy. Not this time. It's—business."

Her eyes turned hard and the two steely glints were back. She opened her mouth to speak, then rushed to the rear of the house. She still vaccilated between trust and trauma at times.

With a sigh I let myself out the front door and went for my car. I'd have to reckon with her later. She was too observant to take along, and this had to be my secret.

The air hung stale and motionless in the carriage-house garage, and I wiped my forehead when I got into the closed car. The day promised to be another scorcher.

My first stop was to see Terri at the hospital lab. I wanted answers so badly. If I could prove Aunt Corrie was being drugged, I'd leave no stone unturned to find out who was responsible. That person was most likely to be the one who wanted her out of the way.

Both Colin and Paul visited Aunt Corrie frequently, and there were other visitors occasionally. It could be someone I didn't even know, someone outside the family. Yet I was convinced someone was tampering with the medication.

I reached the hospital, parked the car, and hurried through the glass doors into the quiet lobby. Glancing at the large-framed directory on the wall, I discovered that the labs were located on the third floor. Nurses and orderlies moved capably through the corridors with supplies and trays in soft, muffled noises that mark a hospital.

I stepped into the elevator and pushed the button for the third floor. At the west end I saw gleaming white walls with an arrow pointing toward a neatly lettered sign that said LABORATORIES. Walking briskly along the shiny tiled floor, I found myself in front of a pair of large double doors.

I pushed them open gently and stepped into a room lined with shelves. Beyond the door stood a large desk.

The middle-aged receptionist looked up from her chair as I came in. "May I help you?"

"I'd like to see Terri Downing, please."

"Who, may I ask, is wanting to see her?"

"Amy Sutton. We're friends. I—I have a message of importance."

She got up and motioned me to follow. "She's in Lab Number Two. We don't usually allow outsiders back here, but I'll do it for Terri, since it's important."

I walked beside her to a large, airy room, sterile with gleaming white tile, tubes, and other laboratory equipment, brilliant under bright fluorescent lights.

Terri sat on a high stool, her head bent over a microscope. She looked professional in her white lab coat and glanced up when we entered.

"Oh, hi, Amy!" she called out. "It's good to see you. What brings you here?" She paused to nod to the receptionist, who turned and left.

I took the aspirin bottle from my purse. "Terri, would you run a test on this medication and tell me what's in it? I suspect someone's trying to keep my aunt sedated, but I'm not sure."

"Why, of course." She took the bottle from me. "I'll have to do that during my off hour, Amy. But I'll let you know what I find as soon as I can."

We exchanged several pleasantries, and I made my way back through the office, down the shiny corridors, and took the elevator down. Minutes later I reached my car.

The heat was bearing down on me, and I stopped to repair my makeup before driving to Daryl Swanson's office. I was eager to hear what he had discovered. He was waiting when his secretary announced me some time later.

"Sit down, Amy—may I call you that? I've been busy since you were here yesterday and I've discovered a few things."

I moistened my lips. "What . . . things?"

"First, I obtained a court order, forcing McDivitt to reveal who your great-aunt's heirs are. Now, are you ready for this?" I noticed a twinkle in his kind gray eyes.

"Oh. . . ." I gasped a bit, then nodded. "Yes, of course. What have you found out?"

"It seems in the original will her three stepchildren and you were to inherit equally. But before the accident she was ready to change her mind. She planned to leave Meriweather Hall to Brandy, since she felt Brandy was the only person who loved her, she said."

"Yes," I said slowly, remembering Brandy's comment about it being "our house." I studied my fingertips absently, then looked up. "I'm sorry it's taken this accident to show us all what Aunt Corrie means to us," I added finally. "I haven't been back in twelve years, and I'm ashamed of it. But my father discouraged my coming back here after my mother died. I think he wanted me to break all ties."

"That's too bad. She really must've loved you to want to leave anything at all to the four of you."

"I know. And I'm more sorry than I can say. That's why I want to make it up to her now, show her love and care because I really do love her. Only, everything's mixed up."

He nodded. "I understand. Although the new will had been drawn up, Corinda Ward hadn't signed it because the accident probably occurred at that time. What do you know about the three stepchildren? Would any of them have reasons for creating problems for her, especially siphoning off her money?"

"I really don't know. Paul has had a heavy load of medical expenses due to his wife's illness, and Colin lives so high that he's always complaining about his lack of money. As for Kathryn, I can't think of a single reason she should want Aunt Corrie's money, with her good job as ace reporter. In fact, she's the one who pays for the medications and some other expenses. So none of this makes sense to me. That's what is so confusing."

"Well," Mr. Swanson said, leaning back in his chair, "under this new arrangement McDivitt has thirty days to give an accounting of her financial status. But with you as her guardian—"

"I wish I wouldn't have to do this, Mr. Swanson," I cut

in. "I don't want the stepchildren on my back!"

"But someone has to, and since you're the only living blood relative and heir—"

"If there were only another way."

"This is the best way, believe me!"

My thoughts roiled. The new will had not been finalized, and as matters stood now, Aunt Corrie's property and money would be equally divided among Paul, Kathryn, Colin, and me at her death. And if they knew I was being made guardian, there were certain to be sparks. But what else was left?

Slowly I got to my feet. "Let me think about this some more," I said, feeling suddenly inadequate and small. "I'll let you know in a few days what I decide."

"Don't wait too long, Amy. Someone must be in charge."

"I know. But it's such a big step. I must be absolutely sure it's what I have to do."

With a word of thanks and good-bye, I left his office and drove home, more upset and depressed than I'd been in days. I realized the problems would multiply, for all accusations could now be heaped upon me, and I wasn't ready for this.

When I got home I dragged into the house, eager for a cold shower and bed. If only I could sleep this nightmare away!

As I started for the stairs, the hall phone rang, and I hurried to answer it.

"Yes? This is Amy Sutton."

The voice at the other end of the line was hoarse with anger. "You—you meddler! You interloper! What gives you the right to interfere in Corinda Ward's affairs?"

"Who—who are you?" I asked, taken aback at the fierce lash of words.

"This is Al McDivitt. You've no right to barge in—"

"I do so have a right," I interrupted. "I'm Corinda Ward's only living blood relative, Mr. McDivitt. I must know what's happening to my great-aunt's money, since you have refused to tell me anything."

"Let me tell you, young woman," he hissed, "you'll be sorry—just very sorry if you go through with this!" The receiver slammed in my ear.

I turned and groped for a chair, then saw Brandy in the doorway, her green eyes wary.

"I hope you don't forget that I live here," she said in a small worried voice. "And that God's here too.'"

For a moment all my other troubles faded. I rushed toward her and scooped her into my arms.

"Oh, Brandy—Brandy!" I murmured against her hair. "I'm sorry. I guess I've been so busy I almost forgot. Yes, I almost forgot."

My faith had been shaken these past few days but suddenly the anchor held fast once again. Pushing aside Brandy's reddish hair, I looked into the green eyes. They were serene, and she smiled at me.

18

Brandy's unexpected response reassured me, and I calmed. I had thought she would be upset because I didn't take her with me, but often a child's anger fades more quickly than an adult's.

Paul eyed me quizzically at the dinner table. "You look bushed, Amy," he said, attacking the roast beef with his knife. "Had a rough day?"

"I—yes, I guess so," I said, not eager to share my reasons.

"Well, summer's almost over and you'll soon be back in your classroom."

Brandy dropped her spoon with a clatter. "No, she's not. She's promised to stay here for a long time. Haven't you, Amy?"

"You—what?" Paul looked straight at me. "But your teaching job. . . ."

I sighed and laid down my fork. "She's right. I called the administration at Peter Conrad today and resigned my position."

"But why? When I asked you to come, I didn't mean for you to give up your own life and devote all this time here with your great-aunt. You know I wouldn't have expected that."

"I know, Paul. But since I've been here, I see so many

things that need my attention. Someone has had to look after things, and I know you can't do it all—especially with Susan being so ill."

"Yes, and I do appreciate all you've done here, Amy. You've taken a big load from my shoulders. I don't know how I'd have managed without you. With Sue. . . . But Amy, for you to give up your own plans. . . ."

"It's what I have to do, Paul."

"And your marriage to Eric Stone postponed. . . ."

"I'm not going to marry Eric."

He looked startled, then regained his composure quickly. "If you gave him up because of what you felt is your duty here, Amy—"

"No, Paul. That had nothing to do with it. I just didn't love Eric with the kind of love that belongs between man and woman."

He looked away, deep pain lurking in his eyes. He was obviously remembering Susan and the crumbling of his own future with the woman he loved.

We finished our meal in silence, for I couldn't bring myself to talk about the subject again. Brandy excused herself and scrambled away from the table, heading toward the back door.

"I know you don't want me to be tied down, Paul. It's just that I felt strongly I should stay—at least until I see the edge of the dawn."

He walked toward the door and paused. Then he turned and looked at me. "Amy, I'm grateful for what you've done for Brandy. She—she's simmered down unbelievably, you know. I realize that you've been responsible for that too."

Laying my napkin aside, I got up from the table. "She's missed her mother, Paul. I've only tried to help fill the

147

void. . . ." I paused, realizing how awkward my words must sound. "I mean, she—she needed someone and I've tried to be available."

"Yes, Amy." His voice was low and gentle. "I—I'll be forever grateful to you for that. I guess what I'm trying to say is, maybe I did the right thing in asking you to come."

"The Lord had a purpose in bringing me here, I'm sure. I'm still not quite certain what it is."

He eyed me whimsically. "I think I'm beginning to understand a little, Amy. Your God seems to know what he's doing."

"You're absolutely right, Paul. And don't you forget it!"

The jangle of the hall phone interrupted our conversation and I hurried to answer it. It was Terri Downing.

"Amy, you were right," she said with a note of excitement in her voice. "There's a good dose of Valium in this medication. Someone obviously has wanted your aunt sedated. It's certainly enough to keep her in a stupor. Who do you suppose has access to a Valium prescription?"

"Anyone might have, Terri. Anyone under a great deal of stress."

I could hardly contain the news. Tomorrow I would confront Dr. Blair with Terri's report. My tiredness vanished and my step was light as I cleared the dinner table and scraped plates for Annie Jane.

"I declare, Miss Amy," she said, "you seem real pert tonight. Your young man going away sure ain't upset you."

I tried to hide a smile. "Well, Annie Jane, sometimes one realizes when things are for the best. I think this was one of them."

When I came through the front hall and started for the stairs, I was surprised to see Colin sitting on the lowest stairstep. His usually merry face was creased into a frown.

"Amy," he said, and the usual bantering tone was missing, "what have you been up to?"

My skin grew cold in the warm evening air at his words. "What do you mean, Colin?"

"Al McDivitt stormed into the bank just before we closed and accused you of siccing Swanson on him. The guy's just livid!"

Paul came up behind me, his face a question mark. "What's up, you two?"

With a sigh I started for the library. "Come and we'll talk," I said in an unsure voice, turning on the lights and fan as I went in. I had hoped to have more time to think about the whole matter before sharing it with the two brothers.

Paul and Colin followed me silently. I sat down on the sofa, and Paul reluctantly took the brown armchair. Colin remained standing, his arms behind his back, his face implacable.

After a quick and silent prayer for guidance, I began. "I know the two of you haven't wanted me to disturb the waters here at Meriweather Hall. But we're all in this together, so I might as well tell you."

Paul's dark face looked drawn and intense, and I couldn't imagine what his thoughts were. Colin seemed a bit uneasy. I noticed his jaw twitch slightly.

"I've told you about visiting Al McDivitt and trying to discover what's happening to Aunt Corrie's money. Both of you deny knowledge of where it's going. Yet you object to my trying to find out! Well, Al McDivitt's right. I talked to Daryl Swanson because I wondered if we could do anything to save what's left. What's wrong with that?"

I noticed the brief look that passed between Paul and Colin, but I couldn't catch the significance of what they were trying to convey.

"Go on," Paul said, and Colin nodded.

Moistening my lips, I went on. "Mr. Swanson says that as Aunt Corinda's only blood relative, I am to be declared her legal guardian. McDivitt is to make an accounting within thirty days, after which the bank will act as conservator." I paused, looking up at Colin.

An amused smile spread over his face. "You—the guardian. Well, I'll be." He shook his tawny head.

Paul stared straight ahead, his look impenetrable.

"Please believe me; I'm doing this only because I'm concerned about her finances," I continued. "The fact that I'm an heir—"

"*You're* the heir." Colin exploded. "What about us?"

"We're all heirs. She's named us equally," I said. "But we inherit only at her death."

Paul looked at me, his gaze softening. "She—she's most generous. After all, we're not of direct relationship."

"No. But that's because she loves you. What bothers me is the fact that someone tried to push her down the stairs, wanted her out of the way."

"You can't prove that!" Colin burst out hotly. "Amy, why do you insist—"

"Maybe I can't prove it, but if she came out of her stupor, she'd be able to tell us, wouldn't she? Yet someone's trying to keep that secret locked away from us."

"What do you mean?" Paul asked, his face suddenly white.

"I have suspected this before, as you both know. Well, this morning I took a sample of her liquid medication to

150

the hospital lab and asked my friend Terri Downing to check it out. She called me back a few minutes ago. The sample was loaded with Valium."

Relief flooded Paul's face at my words, but Colin remained skeptical. "And what does that spell?" he asked dryly.

"Whoever is responsible for the problems around here is trying to keep Corinda Ward from returning to normal," I said.

By now I felt drained. If only I'd had a chance to confront Dr. Blair and find out what he knew about the matter. Perhaps there was some logical explanation.

Colin came and sat down beside me. "Okay, Amy. I can see why you're so upset, and why you insisted on firing McDivitt." He took my hands in his and the bantering look was back in his eyes. "But sweetheart, you may be in bigger trouble than you realize. The guy's a tiger, or I miss my guess."

I withdrew my hands quickly. "Why should Aunt Corrie have trusted him with power of attorney, if that's the case?"

"It goes back to the time when your great-grandfather Meriweather was alive," Paul said. "Al was the accountant for Meriweather Lead and Zinc Mines from the time he got out of business college. He handled the finances then, and I guess she decided to let this continue after our dad died. She probably figured he knew what was best."

"Your father managed her finances?"

"As long as he was alive," Colin put in. "And he did a good job too. After he died—"

"But if you suspected mayhem, why didn't you try to stop McDivitt?" I demanded. "You tried to tell me he was trustworthy!"

Paul shook his head. "It's like I said. She always went over the accounts with him, as long as she was able. She trusted him, so why shouldn't we? If she thought he was mishandling anything, she didn't tell us. But she was generous to a fault, you know."

I nodded, remembering how she had helped Paul with Susan's staggering medical expenses.

"What do we do next?" I said finally. "Shall we go ahead with Mr. Swanson's legal action?"

Paul got up and started for the door. "I'm behind you, Amy."

"How about Kathryn?" I asked. "She needs to know what's going on here, too."

"She'll agree," Paul said. "She'll be relieved with all this, I'm sure."

"I'll tell her," Colin said, helping me to my feet. "Don't worry about Kathryn, Amy. She'll come around."

I went up to my room feeling somewhat relieved. I'd worried how Paul and Colin would take the news of my being made guardian, and it was good to have their approval. I was sure Kathryn would acquiesce, for I'd found her to be a most agreeable person.

Crawling into bed, I lay for awhile, pondering the events of the day. Terri's phone call had climaxed a period of suspicion, of speculation. Now I could lay that aside and concentrate on finding out who had placed the Valium in the medication.

"But it's too much to think about tonight," I murmured into the clean sheets before I turned over and went to sleep.

Fresh, sweet air blew into the east windows the next morning when I awoke. I showered and pulled on a bright, colorful sleeveless sundress. After brushing my short brown hair, I dabbed on a bit of makeup and went downstairs for breakfast.

I found Brandy huddled over the cabinet, pouring milk into her bowl of cereal. She looked up as I came in.

"Guess what," she said airily. "I've thought about it. When we go to see Grandma Corrie this morning, I'm going along and tell her it's okay."

I stopped, startled by her abrupt conversation. "What's okay, Brandy?"

"That Jesus wants to take my momma up to heaven. I know she can't come back here, but I still have Snow White and Aunt Corrie. And you'll be here, so all we need is to wait for Grandma Corrie to wake up. Don't you think?"

Groping for time, I measured my oat bran into the kettle. "Well . . . of course," I said finally. "But what if she—she isn't awake this morning?"

"Oh, she'll wake up some time. Then everything will be okay. When she wakes up you and me and Grandma Corrie will have lots of fun with Snow White, won't we?"

When she wakes up, I'll go away, I told myself. When it happens, *my job here is over.*

"Amy?"

My oat bran made soft, swishy sounds as it bubbled in the kettle. I mustn't let Brandy build up false hopes. What should I say?

"Amy? Aren't you listening?"

"Wha—oh, yes, of course. I . . . was busy with my cereal."

"Well, grown-ups tell me to pay attention, but they don't have to. I hope I'll never grow up." Her green eyes glinted. "Then I won't ever have anything to worry about."

"But children can learn from little worries," I said. "God made us that way. He wants us to trust him, to look to him for help in all things."

"Then why do you worry about what's happened to Grandma Corrie?"

I sighed a little. "Good question, Amy. I'll work it out some way. When she wakes up and my job here is over and I—"

"You won't go away, Amy?" Brandy was perilously close to tears. I saw the green eyes harden.

"Not—not for a long time," I muttered, pouring my cereal into one of the large breakfast bowls. "Be sure to—to check on Snow White. I thought I heard her by the door."

She eyed me slyly, as if doubting the truth of my words. Somehow I had to get her mind off my staying on at Meriweather Hall when I knew I must leave.

The front doorbell rang at that moment and I left my breakfast to answer it. A smiling young man, wearing a natty, light tan suit and crisp white shirt, stood on the other side of the storm door. His hair was styled and shaped in the latest fad, and his handsome face was clean-shaven.

"Yes?" I said.

His smile widened. "You must be Amy. Kathryn's told me all about you. I'm Grant Lawrence. We've never met. May I come in?"

I was startled for a minute. "Oh, I'm sorry. I didn't recognize you. Yes, do come in."

"I hope I'm not too early, but I felt I should come and see you."

Leading the way to the library, I tried to remember what I knew about Grant Lawrence. Not much, I mused. All I knew was that he and Kathryn were separated, and that she seemed unhappy. I assumed he had left Waylan.

"Do sit down," I said, showing him to the sofa. "Brandy and I were in the kitchen finishing our breakfast."

"You're a most remarkable person, Amy," he said, taking the preferred seat. "Giving up your summer plans to look after a sick old woman and keeping the household going."

"Someone had to do it," I said, seating myself opposite him, "so Paul elected me."

"And you'll be leaving soon?" he asked. "Since school is about to begin—"

"I'll stay as long as I'm needed."

"That's very noble of you. Not everyone has such dedication."

I wondered why he had come. Surely he must feel somewhat awkward at Meriweather Hall since he and Kathryn were no longer together.

"Look, Grant," I said rather impatiently, "is there anything I can do for you? I must go upstairs to see my great-aunt . . . ."

"Why, of course. I guess I was a bit presumptuous. You *are* leaving soon, aren't you? I just wanted to meet you."

I thought, He seems anxious for me to leave Meriweather Hall. But why should he? Surely he knows there's nothing here for him without Kathryn.

"If you'll excuse me—" I got to my feet.

He jumped up and walked toward the door. "Of course. Forgive me. In spite of the fact that Kathryn and I are separated, I still have strong feelings about this place. Very strong. I'm trying to persuade my wife to come back to me."

Something about him puzzled me, but I couldn't put my finger on it. He hurried to the front door. I saw him out and breathed a sigh of relief.

155

On the front porch he suddenly whirled around. "If I were you, Amy, I'd go back to California real soon—before you get hurt." With those words he swung into his little Renault and roared away.

His parting words sent a chill up my spine. Was it a threat? He was charming, all right. No wonder poor Kathryn had been taken in by him. But somehow I didn't blame her for not sticking with him.

Slowly I walked up the stairs. My next few moments with Aunt Corrie were as perplexing as ever. She made no sign that she heard a word I read or said. Yet I was more certain than ever that she could come out of her groggy state if the Valium were eliminated. But now I was right back where I started.

Who was to blame?

19

After lunch I dressed hurriedly, backed my car out of the carriage-house garage, and drove down the graveled driveway and onto the highway.

Apart from the August heat the afternoon was pleasant. Only a few high, cauliflower clouds hung motionless in the sky.

I swung into the mainstream of traffic as I headed toward downtown Waylan. A turbid stream of taxis and cars bathed midtown with exhaust fumes and made a grinding, sullen roar.

I pulled into the Waylan Clinic parking lot, checked my purse for the information I had picked up from Terri, and entered the wide, glass-paned doors. The receptionist looked up when I paused before her desk.

"I'm Amy Sutton," I said, "and I wish to see Dr. Blair on a matter pertaining to my great-aunt Corinda Ward. It's extremely important."

She checked the schedule sheet and nodded. "We've had a cancellation. Please be seated, and I'll call you shortly."

About twenty minutes later she called my name. I got up and walked through the door leading into the doctor's suite of offices.

Dr. Blair sat behind his desk, frowning slightly when I came into the consulting room. He motioned me to a chair with a wave of his hand.

"What is it this time, Miss Sutton?" he asked with a touch of irritation. "Is it about Mrs. Ward?"

"Yes," I said, handing him Terri's report.

"What's this about?" he asked, scanning the paper quickly.

"It's a report of Aunt Corrie's medication. I had the hospital lab check it out."

His gaze narrowed at my words. Then he looked at it again. "Valium! This report shows it contains Valium. I've never prescribed any kind of sedative for her!" He studied the paper again, then he handed it back to me abruptly. "There must be some mistake. All I give her is liquid vitamins. Why should I prescribe Valium for her?"

"I don't know. You told me earlier that you didn't sedate her," I said. "But I had the medication tested because I suspected someone was trying to keep my aunt in a stupor."

His eyes softened as he reached for the report again. Studying it more intently, he leaned forward. There was genuine concern in his face.

"You're right, Miss Sutton. Someone is obviously trying to keep my patient from returning to normal." He paused and scratched his head. "Could you know any reason why?'"

"Because she's shown signs of waking up. Whoever is to blame may want to keep her from telling who pushed her down the stairs."

"Yes," he said, nodding. "That's possible."

"Would you have any idea who is responsible?" I asked, the words fairly leaping from my lips.

He drew a deep breath. "If I did, I'd certainly tell you. The only person who handles the medication is Leo Remmick, the pharmacist. He fills the prescription, which I give to Kathryn Lawrence."

"Is this pharmacist reliable?"

"Do you mean, would he have reason to put Valium in the medication? Never. He's totally dependable, one of the best."

My brain reeled. If the doctor had no explanation, what answer was there?

"Is Kathryn the only person who comes in for the—the vitamins?"

"She's the one who picks up the prescription here." He reached for the phone. "Let me dial Leo and ask."

I waited while Dr. Blair talked to the pharmacist. I knew his shop was also under the Waylan Clinic roof. The doctor's words were short and clipped. Then he turned to me again.

"Leo says only Kathryn Lawrence picks up the medication. She also pays for it. Here, I'll give you a fresh prescription for *you* to have filled for your aunt. Remove the other bottle from her room and keep it in a safe place in case it is needed for evidence."

"Thank you, doctor," I said, getting to my feet.

He reached out his hand. "I'm glad you told me. If I can help further in any way, please let me know."

I purchased the medication for my aunt, left the clinic building, and drove home slowly. I was grateful for the doctor's support. Still, something didn't make sense. If Kathryn were the only person who picked up the medication, how did the Valium get there? Kathryn was perfectly innocent. She was as concerned for Aunt Corrie's well-being as I was. Where did her estranged husband Grant fit in? Was there any possible way he could slip the tranquilizer into the bottle? After his strange visit to me yesterday, I was beginning to believe anything.

159

As soon as possible, I'd talk to Kathryn and find out if anyone had a chance to slip Valium into the prescription before she delivered it to Meriweather Hall.

The matter was urgent. The minute I arrived back at Meriweather Hall, I headed for the phone. The sooner I called the Kathryn, the better.

Before I had laid down my purse and picked up the phone book, Brandy burst into the front hall, her green eyes filled with alarm.

"Amy!" she cried, "I can't find Snow White! She—she's absolutely disappeared. I've called and called and looked and looked. She's not *anywhere!*"

Great tears cut wide shiny paths down her freckled cheeks, and I put my arms around her, cradling her head against me.

"There, there," I soothed, "we'll find her. I'm sure she's somewhere."

"Will you help me find her?" she mumbled tearfully, lifting her face.

"You know I will, Brandy, as soon as I change my clothes. Remember, Snow White's special to me too. Why don't you check the barn once more? Maybe she's come back. I'll join you soon."

"Please hurry!" She pulled away from me and rushed toward the rear of the house. I heard the back door slam as I started for the stairs. A car sounded in the driveway, and I decided it was probably Colin or Kathryn.

Changing into jeans, an old plaid shirt, and my garden shoes, I started down the hall. The familiar click-click of Kathryn's high heels sounded on the lower step, and I waited for her at the head of the stairs. She looked cool and precise in her fiery red dress. Sometimes I envied her perfection, her poise.

"Kathryn!" I called out. "You're just the person I want to see."

"Hi!" she said brightly. "You look comfortable. Going somewhere, or toiling in the garden?"

"Snow White's disappeared, and I promised Brandy I'd help find her."

"If I wasn't all gussied up, I'd help you," she said with a whimsical smile. "This might make a cute feature story. Child loses kitten and all that."

We laughed, and as she began to move on I laid a hand on her shoulder. "Kathryn, I've got to tell you something I know will interest you."

"What's up, Amy?"

"It's about Aunt Corrie."

Her face lit up. "You know how much she means to me. Anything wrong?"

"She—she appears to have been drugged, so I took a sample of her medication to Terri Downing at the hospital lab. According to her tests, it's laced with Valium."

"Valium!" she cried. "Are you sure? Maybe she made a mistake. But how in the world—?"

"That's what I aim to find out. Once I do, a great many puzzling questions will be answered."

She turned with a quick lift of her saucy nose. "Isn't that something! Poor Corrie-Mom. How in the world do you s'pose—"

"I don't know. Listen, Kathryn. Grant Lawrence came to see me this morning."

Her gaze narrowed and her tone was low. "What did the stinker want?"

"I don't know. Said he wanted to meet me. But some remarks he made left me wondering how much of all this he knows."

"Believe me, he can charm a snake out of its hole. That man can be absolutely cruel."

"Yes," I said absently. "Kathryn, would—would he have access to the medication?"

"You mean, slip in the Valium? I don't know. He—he's begged me to come back to him but. . . ." She paused, and I saw sudden fear in her eyes.

Poor Kathryn. She certainly had her share of heartaches. If only she'd let the Lord help her, I thought.

I glanced at my watch. "But I'd better run along and help Brandy look for her kitten. She claims she's looked everywhere."

"The little thing couldn't have wandered out toward Old Number Two, could it?" she offered.

"It's an idea," I said. "She followed us once before. I'll check it out right away. See you later." I moved down the stairs and hurried out of the house.

Brandy flew to meet me as I headed toward the barn. "Snow White isn't *anywhere!*" she cried again. "She's just gone!"

"Well, she's got to be somewhere. Have you checked along the stone walls? Remember when Annie Jane told you about Snow White on the wall? Why don't you check? I—I'll take a quick look at the old mine," I said casually, not wanting to frighten her. "You stay right here. I'll be back soon."

After I let myself through the gate, I set off on a jog down the dim trail. One thing I didn't need now was Brandy's panicky presence.

Looking this way and that, calling the kitten's name, I hopped across the meadow, inhaling the sweet fragrance of freshly cut hay. Snow White had followed us once before to the mine, and for some unknown feline reason could have trailed toward the direction of Old Number Two on her own.

A hot breeze blew against my cheeks, and I pushed ahead between thick clumps of grass that gave way to rustling sounds as I trudged between the wheel tracks. My shoes sent up puffs of dust that settled thickly on the grass between the ruts.

"Snow White?" I called over and over. "Snow White! Here, kitty, kitty. . . ." My voice echoed over the fields. No response. The kitten must have remained near the house after all. The path ahead grew more rocky and hilly, and I slowed my pace, debating about turning back.

Just then I thought I saw a flash of white near the mine entrance and I set out on a run. As I neared the boarded-up adit, I could make out the fluffy white shape. The eerie feeling that always settled over me when I came toward the old mine draped its mantle over me now. A peculiar grayness covered the sky and a sudden gust of wind shrieked from the north.

"Snow White!" I yelled again as I saw the little white kitten scamper toward the broken boards that covered the adit.

Reaching out my hands, I stooped to grab her. She eluded me and shot forward, teetering on the brink of the rotting timbers. The opening had already caved in once. Now the barrier of boards had fallen into ruin. The farmer who owned the land should build a tight fence around this dangerous place, I decided. But more and more mines were caving in, and he probably had enough to do without adding this job.

Snow White was chasing a brown leaf that swirled and

eddied in the brisk wind over the open area. I saw her climb nimbly across the rotting timber.

"Snow White!" I screamed. "You naughty kitten!"

Kneeling down, I reached for the wiggling white animal. I had almost reached her when she slithered out of my grasp. She lost her balance and began to roll along one of the broken boards. Throwing myself on my stomach, I thrust out my right hand to grab her before she slid farther down into the opening. By now my head and torso were almost hanging over the edge.

"Snow White, you scamp!" I cried, reaching down for the kitten. I thought I heard a sound behind me. Before I could turn, I felt someone's hands quickly shove my shoulders from behind. With a rattle of gravel and rock, I found myself hurtling through the mine's opening. The descent was not entirely vertical, for the cave-in formed a steep slant. I rolled and bumped down, down, into the darkness, trying to brace myself against resisting heavier clumps of earth, but I was going too fast.

With a sudden thump I came to a stop at the bottom. I sat up and tried to catch my breath. Almost total darkness covered me, with only a faint light seeping from the adit above me. My arms hurt and my body felt bruised and sore, and a sharp pain stabbed my ankle. Somewhere in the gloom around me, I heard the faint mewing sound of the kitten.

Then the full impact hit me: *Someone had deliberately pushed me into the mine!*

20

I rubbed my ankle and blinked my eyes in the dimness, trying to make out some vague shape. Only the dank pungent smell of dark earth permeated the atmosphere. Above me I saw the gaping hole where the opening had caved in. All else was deep gloom. Dirt and gravel had scratched my body as I had tumbled down the slide, and now the scratches stung. I tried to rationalize the situation. If I had rolled down, perhaps there was a way up. But what of Snow White? I couldn't leave her down here. I saw a faint white blur about ten feet to my left, and moving forward painfully, I groped for the ball of fluff.

"Here, kitty!" I called again. "Come, Snow White."

When I reached out to touch her she whisked away. You'd think she'd recognize me as a friend, I thought, someone to save her, someone for a companion. Apparently she could see in the dark better than I. At least, cats were supposed to possess that instinct.

The cave-in seemed steeper than I thought when I limped back to the incline and tried to scale the almost perpendicular wall. Digging in my toes, I tried to claw my way up the slant, but the pain in my ankle sent me crumpling to my knees.

With a sigh of desperation I sat down to rest. Maybe after I caught my breath and my heart stopped pounding, I'd think of another way out.

Besides, Kathryn and Brandy knew where I was. Surely someone would come out and check, and I would be rescued.

Trying to reconstruct the moment I had leaned over the edge of the crumbling adit, I recalled again the sensation of being pushed. Who would have dared do such a thing? Brandy? She had pushed me down from the haymow floor once, and she could do it again. Yet that was before she began to accept me and trust me. A few days ago she had begged me to stay. Even Paul had sensed her change of feeling toward me. For her to shove me into the dark mine didn't make sense.

"Mew . . . mew. . . ." Snow White was making small sounds as she crept along the blackest side of the cavelike room.

My ankle was beginning to throb more intensely. Even if I could inch my way up the slide, the pain would cramp my efforts to find my way out.

If only I could let Brandy know where I was. She was sure to look for me if I didn't return. I decided to call out —to let someone know I was thirty or forty feet down in the drift. I vaguely recalled words Great-grandpa Meriweather used to tell me in his stories about the mines. *Drift* was the tunnel where the blasting and shoveling was done. The *stope* in the drift was the other end, where shovelers picked up their ore. The stope was upward toward the *headin'*, where new rock was blasted. But nothing of all this helped me now.

"Help. . . . Help!'" I screamed until I was hoarse. My voice echoed through the hollow drift and bounced back. Would my screams reach open air? How long had I been in this gloomy place? Five minutes? Ten? It seemed like an hour.

Rubbing my ankle, I leaned back. I hadn't given Brandy enough time to reach the mine, and I settled back to think through the situation. Only Brandy and Kathryn knew where I had gone, and I had ruled out Brandy as having pushed me. That left only Kathryn. But that was absurd. Kathryn was the last person I suspected of mayhem. Even if Colin—or Paul—had come home unexpectedly and Brandy had told them where I'd gone, I couldn't believe either of them would do this. Hadn't both assured me just yesterday that they backed me in my search for answers?

Then the thought I'd tried to push from my mind surfaced. Had Grant Lawrence returned for some reason? Was he responsible for this?

Pain throbbed in my ankle and I strained my ears for any sound in the unearthly silence of my prison. Only the faint whimpering sounds of the kitten came through the darkness. My mind reeled. Oh, why couldn't I find answers? It *had* to be Grant.

But why? What was behind all this? I recalled his veiled threat just this morning. Kathryn had seemed disturbed that Grant had been to see me. I saw the fear in her face when I told her. What was she trying to hide? What was she afraid of? Kathryn couldn't possibly be behind this whole business. *Or could she?*

The thought hit me like a thunderbolt. It was *Kathryn* who bought Aunt Corrie's medication. She would have the perfect chance to tamper with it. She'd been under so much stress with her marriage problems. Possibly she was taking Valium to cope with them. Yet why should she want Aunt Corrie out of the way? I was more confused than ever.

"Mew . . . mew . . . mew. . . ."

Somewhere in the vague dimness beyond I heard Snow White's pitiful sounds, and I stirred restlessly. If only I could catch her and get us both back on solid ground.

Thoughts of Kathryn persisted. She had been pleasant and congenial. Yet there were times when she seemed disturbed about my news of Aunt Corrie's apparent signs of recovery. I recalled a conversation with Colin in which he'd intimated that Kathryn had sometimes pretended to be Cinderella and Aunt Corrie the wicked stepmother. But that was years ago. Wasn't Kathryn paying for the medication now? She seemed genuinely concerned for her stepmother. And yet—

I shook myself. I was growing morbid, shut away in this dank hole with no foreseeable way of escape.

In the shadowy darkness I listened to the pathetic mewling of Brandy's pet kitten, and I sat up straighter. Wasn't it about time Brandy came with help?

"I'm here!" I screamed again. "Down here . . . in the mine!" My words echoed through the hollow corridors and died away. Would anyone hear me?

Tears streamed down my cheeks, and I wiped them away with the back of my hand. What am I doing here, Lord? Where are *you?*

Panic welled up inside of me and I fought it, clawing and gritting my teeth in fear. Then slowly I relaxed and began to pray.

"Oh, Lord, I don't know what's happening to Aunt Corrie now—and to me and to us all. But I trusted you to help me through this. I can't believe I've failed and this is all a dead end. I know you brought me to Meriweather Hall and I believed it was for a purpose, to help Brandy, yes. But also to —to help Aunt Corrie through her ordeal. . . . Lord, guide me, please!" My prayer ended in a deep sob.

"*They that wait upon the Lord. . . .*" I had repeated the words so often to Aunt Corrie, begging her to believe them. Could I accept them now for myself? *Wait.* The word hammered into my head like a mine tool to zinc. The Lord had never failed me, and he wouldn't now. I *had* to believe that.

The silence in the murky cavern seemed ominous and more pronounced. Yet my fears had lifted. Whatever happened to me didn't matter, as long as Aunt Corrie and Brandy survived. I moved restlessly, every muscle a bundle of aching.

Stillness seemed to saturate the abandoned mine like a vacuum when it suddenly hit me: I no longer heard Snow White's pitiful mewling noises. What had happened to Brandy's pet kitten?

21

Had Snow White found a way out? But there was no way she could climb up the slide. What had happened to Brandy's pet? I knew the child would be heartbroken if her cat were never rescued.

Like a forgotten melody a line from Great-grandfather Meriweather's journal flitted through my mind: *Main entrance on No. 2 in side of hill for the drift but need vertical shaft for ore removal. . . .*

This was Mine No. 2, which meant an entrance had been made from the side of the hill. Had Snow White found it?

Excitement budded down my spine as I tried to assess my position. I believed I was near the east end of the shaft, the stope in the drift, which meant that the sloping side of the hill was just beyond. The other entrance had to be out in an easterly direction to make contact with the side of the hill. I must feel my way around and try to discover the other opening.

Gritting my teeth against pain, I crawled on my hands and knees to the left, where I'd tried to catch Snow White earlier. Dirt and gravel scraped against my cuts and bruises, but I moved forward. This was probably where the *tub* or bucket, container holding the ore, had been located. Now it was all gone, of course. There was a slight unexpected bend in the tunnel, and as I rounded its curve I noticed a small patch of daylight. *I had found the entrance in the side of the hill!*

How I inched along those last ten feet or so I'll never know, but the way seemed interminable. The boarded-up opening let in enough light for me to see where I was going.

Before I reached the opening I heard a sudden cracking sound, as though someone was tearing the boards away from the side adit. When the last board splintered, I heard a shout.

"She's here, Brandy! Amy's here!"

Strong, tender arms pulled me through the opening and lifted me to my feet in broad daylight. As I blinked in the bright sun, I saw Paul, his dark face creased with worry and anxiety, and I collapsed in his arms. His hold tightened around me and his slender fingers stroked my dirt-matted hair. It was so good to be out.

"Amy, you knew I'd come, didn't you?" Brandy, tugging at my arm, looked at me, her green eyes soft and sad. "You knew I wouldn't leave you in there, didn't you?"

In her other arm she cuddled Snow White, and I was glad to know the kitten was safe. Paul continued to stroke my disheveled hair, then led me to the shady area beside the hill and eased me onto the grass. I noticed the scratches on my arms and touched my cheeks, which burned and flamed as the wind blew around the hillside.

"I must look a sight," I said with a short, apologetic laugh. "It all happened so fast—" My words stopped. What had Brandy meant when she said she wouldn't leave me "there"? Had she pushed me after all?

"Never mind how you look," Paul said, kneeling in front of me. He drew off my shoes, emptied the dirt out of them, and put them back on.

171

"Brandy . . . I don't understand. Someone—someone pushed me. Where—how did you know?" I stammered.

She squatted beside me, stroking Snow White's dirty fur. "I saw her. She—came flying down the trail after you. I followed her, but I was scared she'd see me so I hid behind those big limestone rocks by the dead tree."

"Who, Brandy? Whom did you see?"

"Kathryn. She came close just as you reached for Snow White, then she—she pushed you down. Didn't you see her?"

"Kathryn?" The word seemed to stick in my throat. "No, I . . . didn't see anyone." It was so good to lie back and rest in the cool shade of the hill on the soft meadow grass. I closed my eyes and took a gentle breath. Right now, nothing mattered except knowing Brandy hadn't pushed me.

"Amy. . . ."

I heard Paul's voice and I opened my eyes. His face was full of deep concern. "Amy, I'm so thankful you're safe. When Brandy came back and told me—"

"Look, Paul," I cut in, "please start at the beginning. I guess I'm not sure what's happened during this past hour or so. I don't understand. Why were you home at this time of day?"

He sat down beside me and drew my head against his shoulder. I noticed he was wearing his work uniform and the faint odor of grease and machinery clung to the blue threads. A cloud seemed to pass over his features. He looked so weary.

"There was a—a phone message that called me home about half an hour after you had left to look for Snow White. I no more than came into the house when Brandy dashed up to me and told me everything. I stopped only

172

long enough to call Colin, then started after you. Brandy told me she had followed you after you reminded her to check the stone fence for Snow White. She saw Kathryn hightailing after you, and saw my sister . . . push you . . . saw you disappear. . . ." His voice broke.

"Then after Kathryn had gone . . . back, she came out of hiding and hurried to the house to tell me. I remembered there was another entrance to Old Number Two down the hillside and was just tearing away the boards when Snow White tumbled out. Shortly after, I saw you crawling along."

"Oh, Paul—it's all so mixed up! I never dreamed your sister was behind all this."

"But why would Kathryn want to push you down here?" he asked, his dark eyes incredibly aflame with frustration and dismay.

I drew away from his comforting shoulder. "Don't you see, Paul? She must have been behind all that's happened here at Meriweather Hall. She put Valium into Aunt Corrie's medication to keep her in a stupor so that my great-aunt couldn't identify whoever had pushed her down the stairs."

"My sister!" His words were hoarse. "I find that hard to believe."

"So do I," I said, flicking dirt from my clothes. "There's still so much we don't know, but maybe we'll find answers now. Why would she do it? I've got to find out!"

As I struggled to my feet, Paul picked me up in his arms. "You're in no shape to walk home. Here, let me carry you."

We were silent as Paul carried me down the narrow path toward the old brick mansion. Brandy had already raced ahead, her kitten snuggled against her.

The afternoon was waning and already the sun had moved toward the west and was beginning its descent. The heat was motionless, for the earlier gusts of wind had died down, turning the low clouds in the west to purple-blue.

I was eager to get back to the house for a shower and a change, for I felt filthy and putrid. Most of all, I needed to clear my head.

When Paul carried me through the door, Colin was nervously pacing back and forth in the front hall.

"Amy!" he almost shouted when Paul gently set me down on a hall chair. "You look awful! Brandy just popped in and told me what's happened." Then his usual merry face darkened. "I was afraid of that."

"Afraid of what Colin?" Paul whirled on him. "What do you know about this?"

"Not much. I only suspected Kathryn had some connection, and I've already called the police."

"Where is she?" Paul demanded, his dark face aflame. "Wait until I get my hands on that girl." He knelt down and gently removed my shoes. I flexed my toes, thankful there was no pain, although my ankle had swollen badly.

"She was gone by the time I got here," Colin went on. "The police will pick her up. She can't get far. I told them to bring her by here first."

Paul turned to me. "Would you like to go upstairs and lie down? Colin and I'll handle things here."

"Thank you, Paul, but I want to be here when Kathryn gets back. If you'll ask Annie Jane to help me clean up a bit, I'll come back down."

"Sure."

He hurried toward the kitchen and returned presently with the elderly woman. She gasped when she saw me.

"Oh, Miss Amy! Let's get you cleaned up quick."

Paul picked me up and carried me upstairs to my room, Annie Jane following. He laid me on the bed, turned on the fan, then left.

I sighed as Annie Jane drew off my dirty clothes and got a duster from my closet.

"We'd better get you into the tub, Miss Amy, then I'll rub lotion on them scratches. You'll need a doc to look at the ankle too."

"Later. Right now, I want to get into something fresh and clean and be downstairs when the police come back with Kathryn."

"Suit yourself," she said, shrugging a little.

I limped toward the bathroom, leaning on her arm, and as she turned on the faucet with tepid water, I slipped out of my duster and eased myself carefully over the side of the tub. The water felt cool and refreshing as I drew the washcloth over my sore, aching body.

Some fifteen minutes later I donned a simple blue cotton shift with a multicolored belt and put on a pair of soft terry cloth slippers. Colin waited in the hall to assist me down the stairs.

I heard voices in the library as he helped me into the large room, bright with late afternoon sunshine.

Kathryn slumped in the brown velvet chair, her slender legs crossed demurely. A policeman stood behind. When she saw me she drew in her breath sharply.

Paul stood next to the mantel, his arms folded across his chest, his face clouded.

As Colin helped me to the sofa, Paul turned to his sister. "Okay, Kathryn, let's have it. If you're behind this inane mess, we have a right to know about it!"

She glanced up at the policeman, and I saw how white and scared she looked. He nodded.

"Your family has a right to know. But you'd better get a lawyer before any of this goes further."

She made a feeble little noise in her throat, and I was sure she was trying to stifle a sob.

"It—it was Grant and his gambling that started it. He'd run up a huge pile of gambling debts and his creditors were hounding him. There was no way to pay them. That's when he badgered me about asking Corrie-Mom for the money. For weeks he threatened me if I didn't. I—I had to think of something."

She paused, and I saw her struggle to control her emotions. Then she went on. "That's what happened last May when I was here. She and I were heading down the hall and had reached the top of the stairs. I had begged and pleaded her for money, but she refused. She said she couldn't condone Grant's actions. He was responsible for himself, and paying off these bills wouldn't stop him from gambling. He'd be back for more—and more.

"I knew she was right, but I was scared of Grant. When she kept saying no, I grew angry and grabbed her arm and shook her. She yelled, 'No, no, don't do that!' I had no intention of pushing her, but with my shaking she lost her balance and down she flew. If I hadn't been so furious, I might have grabbed her. When I saw her lying on the landing, I panicked. I was so sure no one had seen me, so I hurried away before anyone knew I was here."

Pausing, she bit her lip sharply and shuddered. "I didn't mean to hurt her! When Annie Jane found her and she lay in the hospital all those weeks and we didn't know if she'd live or die, I felt just awful. But as long as she didn't regain consciousness, my secret was safe.

"Then Grant kept coming on so hard that I feared he'd kill me if I didn't do something. That's when I went to Al McDivitt and begged him to give me the money. It must've been early May. At first he flatly refused. He told me that at her death we'd all inherit equally, and maybe she'd die and I'd have the money from her estate. He also told me she had planned to change her will and leave it all to Brandy. But when she didn't die, I panicked. I had to keep her from signing the new will and from telling what she knew."

We all listened in stunned silence to her confession. Then Paul left the fireplace and marched in front of her chair, thrusting his face next to hers.

"How in the world did you persuade McDivitt to turn loose? Because, that's what he did, isn't it?"

She cowered under his hard gaze. "At a convention I covered in Philadelphia last winter I saw Al with a woman. She wasn't his wife. They looked cozy together. I had him over a barrel and told him if he wouldn't give me the money—*in cash*—I'd tell his wife. He had no choice. Grant's debts had already mounted to over $50,000. There were more later, just like Corrie-Mom said." Her voice was low, and I saw fear and frustration in her eyes.

Colin and I looked at each other, and Paul returned to his stance beside the mantel. We were all somewhat in shock, for we knew the rest. When Aunt Corrie didn't die, Kathryn had to resort to keeping her sedated so she wouldn't identify the person who'd been with her when she fell down the stairs. And she'd probably decided to shut me up when I discovered her secret. That's why she'd hurried after me this afternoon and pushed me into the mine.

She whirled on me now. "Amy, why did you have to go after that Valium bit?" she lashed out. "You'd have been safe if you'd let well enough alone!"

The policeman took her arm. "All right, Mrs. Lawrence. It's time to take you in and book you. We've got plenty on you."

She threw one wild stricken look at her brothers. Both Colin and Paul turned away as the officer led her out of the room.

The library seemed as silent as old abandoned Number Two, except for the lazy tick-tacking of insects in the old maples outside the window.

Finally Colin spoke, his usually merry voice suddenly tired. "I suspected something was going on, but had no idea what. I couldn't be a traitor to my own sister, you know. That's why I resisted your prying at first, Amy, when I figured you were digging into what wasn't your business."

I nodded. "I understand, Colin. And you Paul?"

He came and sat down on the brown chair and faced me. "I was scared that Brandy was the one who'd pushed her. She was always moody and full of surprises in those days, especially if she was crossed. I figured as long as we didn't probe too deeply the secret would remain hidden. And I had so much on my mind with Sue. . . ."

A long weary sigh escaped me. What a network of intrigue had enmeshed the family at Meriweather Hall because of Kathryn's mistake in marrying that handsome scoundrel, Grant Lawrence! I had always admired her poise, her precision in all she did, and it hurt me to think she'd been caught in this web of deceit. Finally it was all over.

The three of us sat quietly with our thoughts. I had no idea what either Colin or Paul were thinking, for they were still, but both must have felt deeply hurt at their sister's misdeeds.

Then I remembered Paul having mentioned something at the mine about being summoned home by a phone call. I turned to him.

"Paul, about the phone call you mentioned earlier. Was it —was it something we should know?"

He dropped his head into his hands. I saw his shoulders shake for a few moments, and he choked back a sob.

"It was the clinic. Sue . . . passed away suddenly early this afternoon," he said, without raising his head. "She— she was so weak. . . ." His body shook with sobs.

Susan gone! And instead of giving in to his own grief, Paul Ward had shouldered the grim situation we'd all shared this hot August afternoon here at Meriweather Hall.

Colin hurried to his brother and knelt down beside him, placing a hand on the quaking shoulder.

"Steady, ol' buddy," he said, his voice full of compassion.

My heart ached as I witnessed Paul's grief. What could I say? All the time when he'd come to my rescue and had shared the agony of his sister's dilemma, he had shoved aside his personal crisis in order to be available to those who needed him. What a man!

I was glad Brandy had gone out to play with her kitten and wasn't there to see her grief-stricken father. The Lord in his mercy had spared her this.

After a few moments Paul wiped his eyes with a clean white handkerchief and sprang to his feet, a faint smile on his lips.

"You know, the last visit Brandy and I made to Sue, she looked so radiant, so alive. I knew she was miserable with chest pain and she was so weak she could hardly speak. But she said, 'Don't grieve for me, Paul. If it hadn't been for Corrie-Mom's precious sharing of the gospel, I'd be afraid to die. But I'm not.'

"When I heard her say that, it seemed all the barriers that had reared their ugly heads through the past years were suddenly swept away for me. It was slow in coming— my way to belief, but God's Spirit never gave up.

"And then there you were, Amy, your faith, and the way you demonstrated it over and over. By giving up your summer, your trip to the Caribbean, your teaching job, to stay and shoulder my responsibilities. And the change in Brandy because you cared about her. I saw God at work, and realized he doesn't make mistakes. That he has a plan for each life, if we're willing to wait for him to reveal it. I— Amy, I want you to know I've decided to follow this great God of yours!"

His dark eyes shone, and I noticed a tear form in Colin's blue eyes. Suddenly I knew why I had come back to Meri-weather Hall. It was to help God fulfill his plans.

22

A lonely, scorching wind moaned over the old gray slabs in the cemetery and flapped the canopy of the tent that stood over Susan Ward's grave. It stirred the dried grasses on the ground, and I trembled as I stood beside Colin in the shade. We were at the rear of the group that had gathered for the committal after the service in the church on the hill. Sprays of fresh flowers, their petals already browning in the wind, smothered the grave site.

I stole a brief glimpse of Paul and Brandy, standing close together near the clodded mound before the closed casket. What were they thinking?

The conviction that Susan's death was a victory came back to me now as the minister read the final words: "I am the resurrection, and the life: he that believeth in me, though he were dead, yet shall he live: and whosoever liveth and believeth in me shall never die. . . ."

If funerals serve any purpose other than to enrich undertakers, they are for the living, not the dead. If there is any comfort in them, it is in the gathering of friends and loved ones. And in the beauty and strength of music and Scriptures affirming the Christian faith. I was glad for the sake of Paul and Brandy that so many friends had come to share their final moments with Susan.

The little girl pulled away from Paul's fatherly arm and

glanced around wildly. When she spied me at the rear, she rushed toward me and threw her arms around my waist, crying as though her heart was breaking.

I ached for her. She was so young to experience the finality of death of one so near and dear to her. All I could do was hold her close, to let her know I was there. She gulped out great sobs that wrenched from her chest, and I patted her gently and murmured soothing words of comfort.

Suddenly she stopped crying and thrust up her tear-washed face. "I hope you'll never, ever go away, Amy. My momma said God sent you here to love me. You've got to stay!"

Dear God, I prayed, I can't stay here forever. What shall I say? I tacked on a smile and drew a tissue from my purse.

"Here, let's dry your eyes, Brandy. I won't go away for a long time, and that's a promise. We still have a job to do for Grandma Corrie, don't we? To pray for her and to 'wait upon the Lord' to wake her up. I want you to put on a happy face next time you visit her."

"Will she be awake when I see her?" she ventured after a sniffly blow with the tissue.

"I don't know. Remember, we're to 'wait upon the Lord.' When he says it's time, she'll look at you just the way you see me right now!"

She seemed satisfied, and hurried back to join her father.

Colin touched my arm and whispered, "You almost have me believing it too."

"I guess you mean about Aunt Corrie," I said slowly. "Who can say? Faith is the substance of things hoped for, you know."

"That's from the Bible, isn't it? Paul seems to have discovered something during his long ordeal with Sue."

"What do you mean, Colin?"

"Oh, he's really been up the wall these past years, especially when she became so ill. But recently he's relaxed, at ease. I'm still trying to figure out what it is."

I eyed him tenderly. "He's turned it over to the Lord, I think. That's where his strength comes from now."

At that moment the small group of family members under the canopy began to move away. The formal words were said, and the body committed to earth. There were handclasps of comfort for Paul and Brandy as people filed past them. Most of Susan's family who had come for the service needed to leave for a long ride home. Colin and I waited on the sidelines until the last carful left, then started with Paul and Brandy for Colin's Porsche.

The drive back to Meriweather Hall was short. After dropping us off, Colin left to go back to the bank and his job. One chapter of life was closed, and it was time to pick up where it left off.

The calendar on my desk caught my eye as I changed from my navy-figured dress with its neck ruffle into a summer cotton. My ankle felt fine. The doctor had assured me it was only a mild sprain. School was less than two weeks away and it was time to check Brandy's wardrobe for clothes.

When I started for her door, she came out wearing her nondescript pink playsuit.

"Looks like we both decided to get comfortable," I said whimsically.

The green eyes lit up. "Oh, yes. It's time to tell Snow White about Momma and the beautiful garden where she sleeps," she said, eager to be on her way.

I stopped her with my hand on her arm. "That's good. Snow White has probably missed you all morning. When you've told her, why not come back here? You and I have things to talk about."

"What things?" The glint in her eyes became wary.

"Oh, school things. Do you realize it's time to get you ready for the fourth grade? You've grown like a weed this summer."

"Oh, but I don't want to go to school. With you here, and Snow White to play with, I think I'd better just stay home."

"No such luck, Brandy," I chided her. "Now run along to your kitten and hurry back."

She threw me an impish grin and rushed away. "I'll be back soon," she called out over her shoulder.

When I looked over her clothes in the closet, I saw that this was an area which needed my immediate attention. Still, I felt a bit helpless. How does an outsider, a non-mother like me, choose the right clothes for a child?

After lunch we made out a list of things she needed. I knew I had to show the list to Brandy's father. He would have the last word about all this. I was rather reluctant to face him so soon after he had buried part of his life, yet I knew it must be done. It didn't seem proper to do it today, but tomorrow he planned to go back to work and time was running out before Brandy's first day of the fall semester.

When Paul came out of his room for dinner, I expected him to look drawn and tired. Instead, he seemed calm, and only faint shadows ringed his deep brown eyes.

"Thanks for being here, Amy," he said when we sat down at the table, waiting for Brandy. "I appreciate all you've done for my daughter. It's made it so much easier for her."

"Perhaps," I said with a quick smile. "Now if you can get her ready for school. . . .' I gave him the list I had put together.

He glanced at it, then handed it back with a sigh, shuddering a little.

"What am I to do with this, Amy? Last year Corrie-Mom helped Sue. Now—" A spasm crossed his face.

"If you'd like me to—"

"Would you, Amy?" he cut in eagerly. "But you've done so much already. It would be another burden—" He paused awkwardly. "All I've done since you got here is dump responsibility on you. It's not fair to you."

"When my job here is over, I'll leave and you can run things to suit yourself," I said with a lightness I didn't feel.

"You mean—when Corrie-Mom wakes up." His words sounded like a confident affirmation.

At that moment Brandy stormed through the door, and Annie Jean brought in the platters of cold cuts and salads that well-meaning friends had left at the house during the afternoon.

"Brandy, after dinner you and I must stop by Aunt Corrie's room for our visit. We missed out on our time with her this morning," I told her.

Paul looked up from the wedge of cheese he placed methodically over a slice of dark bread. "I'd like to join you, if you don't mind. I haven't seen much of her these past few days, with all the—the arrangements."

"I hope the three of us barging in on Mrs. Crosby won't get her dander up," I said with an amused smile.

"Don't worry. I'll handle her if it does."

After we had finished the meal Brandy helped me clear the table, then grabbed my hand as we headed for the stairs. When we started down the upper hall she dropped my hand.

"I'll get your Bible, Amy," she called out, slamming through the door of my bedroom.

"Okay, I'll wait."

I noticed Paul behind me, his gaze curious. "You do this every day, don't you?"

"Oh, we're still trying. Maybe one of these days. . . ." I paused awkwardly.

"The miracle will come," he finished, and I saw the light of faith in his eyes.

When Mrs. Crosby opened the door to our knock, she frowned.

"I hope you don't all expect to come in at once," she grunted.

"That's exactly what we plan to do," Paul told her, and she moved aside somewhat grudgingly to let us in.

I took the chair beside Aunt Corrie's bed as usual and Brandy pulled out the low stool. Paul stood at the foot of the bed. Aunt Corrie lay white and still, her eyes closed.

"We're here, Aunt Corrie," I said softly, "ready for our visit. Remember our special verse?" I added, paging through my Bible to Isaiah 40.

When I was ready to read, I saw the translucent lids flicker and she opened her eyes. A sudden smile lit up her face. With effort she raised her head and reached out a thin white hand.

" 'They—they that . . . wait upon the Lord. . . .' " The words came slowly, yet well articulated. "I thought you'd never get here! I've waited . . . so long, Amy. I'm . . . so glad . . . you're here. Please don't leave me, now that you've come!"

186

She spoke clearly, a faint color dyeing her white cheeks.

"I . . . won't leave—for a long time," I choked out, my heart too full for words.

"Are you here, Brandy?" she called.

With a squeal Brandy jumped up, bent over the frail figure on the bed, and threw her arms around the thin neck.

"I knew you'd wake up, Grandma Corrie! I asked God every day, and he did it," she cried.

By now tears streamed from my eyes and ran down my cheeks. I tried to fight them back. This day had been so full of pain, and now there was joy. At last—at long last Corinda Ward had been released from her nebulous prison, and like the dawn seeping over the edge of the horizon, I realized the answer to my prayers.

Glancing up quickly, I looked at Paul and saw the muscles of his face taut, as though trying to battle his own tears. This was a precious moment, and I was glad he and Brandy were here to share it with me.

At a sound in the doorway, I turned. Mrs. Crosby stood there, formidable in her ill-fitting white uniform, but for the first time I saw a smile break over her flabby face.

23

The old rope swing creaked in the sharp gusts of November wind. I pulled Aunt Corrie's old navy jacket closer around me as I swayed gently back and forth. Dry brown leaves scuttled under the ancient elms across the tawny lawn and whirled away in a dervish dance along the worn path that led toward the front of the house. Tamarisk vines on the gray stone fence flamed with rich scarlet, and overhead a V-shaped flock of wild geese honked southward.

A purple haze drifted over the landscape. The air was like fresh apple cider. I heard the soft *scritch-scritch* of the garden rake as Harry Hill bent his thin, lanky frame to clear away the accumulation of debris in the large yard. Already the place looked less disheveled and shabby since workmen had come to mend shutters, trim shrubs and trees, and set things right at Meriweather Hall.

A fresh blast of wind swooped over the yard, then died away quickly. The long afternoon was growing late, and the sun shone pale through thin clouds in the west.

I was all packed and ready to leave in the morning. My work was done, and I felt a sudden sense of relief. Yet I dreaded the long ride back to California. I was grateful that Paul and Brandy would remain with Aunt Corrie here at Meriweather Hall. With the help of Mrs. Crosby and Annie Jane, my great-aunt was in good hands. She had been coming downstairs for her meals for more than two weeks now, and was making progress every day. But it bothered me when she cried and begged me to stay.

"Now that you've finally come back, I don't want you to go away," she pleaded tearfully when I told her a few days ago.

I had been offered a teaching position in my home school to begin in another two weeks, filling in for a teacher who had asked for a five-month leave to have her baby. It was now or never. I decided it had to be now.

We had told Aunt Corrie as little as we felt was necessary about Kathryn's role in the fall down the stairs, but she was sharper than we gave her credit for.

One day when Brandy and I were with her in the library, she had talked about Kathryn.

"She made me fall, didn't she? She was here, begging me for money to bail her scoundrel husband out of his gambling mess. I had to say no. Poor Kathryn! She always had a temper, you know, and when she pushed her hand against me, I lost my balance. I remember telling her not to do it."

Brandy, busy with her homework at the corner table, looked up. "I remember, too. I was in my room and heard talking on the stairs, but I didn't know who was here. Then I heard the bumpety-bump. . . . When I found Aunt Corrie—"

"*You* found her?" I echoed. Poor child!

"Both Annie Jane and me saw her at the same time, I guess, after we heard the bouncing and thudding. Nobody was around when we got there. I wanted to tell somebody about the voices, but I was afraid. I couldn't forget 'bout it though."

"You did right, Brandy, when you told me," I said. "But why did you tell me?"

"That's because I knew it wasn't you that did it. But when you came, Amy, I was scared you'd find out, and I wanted you to leave. I was scared of whoever it was. Still, I had to tell somebody."

Aunt Corrie winked at her. "Don't tell me you really wanted our Amy to go away," she teased.

"Oh, I don't know. I liked Amy but I didn't want to like her. Why should she be here when Momma. . .?" With a sigh she turned back to her books.

"I suppose Kathryn's in jail for what she tried to do to me," Aunt Corrie went on in a low voice. "Poor Kathryn. Promise me you'll visit her for me, Amy, and tell her I still love her. And that God loves her too. That what she almost did—well, it could've happened to anyone."

"I'll tell her," I promised.

That same week I had seen the precise, perfect reporter in the visitors room at the county jail, her usual poise missing. She looked gaunt and distraught, and her cloud of chestnut hair needed a good brushing. She laced and unlaced her fingers as we talked.

"Aunt Corrie said to tell you she loves you," I told her, and she dropped her gaze to the toes of the sensible brown shoes, so unlike her usual high heels.

When she looked up, her face was stricken. "She always had everything and we had nothing! It wasn't fair. Why couldn't she have shared with us?" Her words were bitter.

Shared with us? I smiled. Who could've done more than Corinda Ward? I had hoped to tell Kathryn about God and his love, but I knew she wouldn't listen now. I went back to Meriweather Hall with a heavy heart.

Paul and Colin and I had had many talks about Corinda Ward and her future. Her finances had straightened out since there was no longer a drain on her funds, with both Kathryn and Grant facing sentences for extortion and embezzlement. Al McDivitt confessed to making a bad investment which had accounted for an earlier loss of her funds. At that time the gardener had to be dismissed and there was no money for repairs on the mansion.

Colin and I had gone over her accounts with her. When she remembered some forgotten stocks, there was enough money to make her financially secure for a long time. She'd been so embarrassed at not knowing where they were. But when she described the brown envelopes, I recalled seeing them in old journals stashed in the hall closet and found them without trouble.

"Colin will help you with your bank statements," I told her when she bewailed Al McDivitt's mishandling of her funds. "And he'll do a good job, too. Why do you need a guardian?"

"You're absolutely right," she said with a burst of her old spirit. "I'll keep a sharp eye on Colin!" Her blue eyes twinkled. "Amy, you have your own life to live, and I realize now that I have no right to keep you here. But it's been so good to have you back."

"That's not it," I told her. "There's not enough for me to do here. You can handle Brandy better than I ever could."

"But you got her straightened out, Amy."

"She was mighty troubled about her mother's illness, which made her unhappy and unsure of herself. With the Lord's help I was available when she needed someone. You'd have accomplished the same thing in time."

Now as I recalled all these discussions, one thing still

191

troubled me. I hadn't had the courage to tell Brandy I was leaving in the morning. I didn't want to upset her. Yet I knew she must be told. I was trying to think of the best way.

She had responded to school well, for which I was glad. Her father was spending more time with her on weekends, taking her to church picnics and school functions.

When I looked at the total picture, I knew the time for me to leave was now. I had fulfilled my obligations, yes, but with more joy than a sense of duty. I couldn't deny that it had been a most difficult summer. And with the problems solved, there was no need for me to stay. So I was delighted with the offer to return to teaching.

Except for one thing: I loved Paul Ward with all my heart. Finally I admitted it to myself. Seeing him every day while he quietly grieved for his wife was hard. Surely the Lord had sent the teaching job my way at the right time.

The swing seemed to move back and forth steadily, and I wondered if the wind was rising again. Then I realized someone was pushing the swing from behind. When I turned, Paul stood there, serene and confident, more relaxed than I'd seen him in months.

Higher and higher the swing moved, and as I hung onto the ropes, the sheer joy of it that I remembered as an eleven-year-old surged through me. For fully five minutes Paul Ward pushed the swing back and forth, then gradually let it die away.

When it stopped he walked toward one of the old elm trees and leaned against it. "Well, that was like old times, wasn't it?" he said with an amused grin.

"Yes, it was," I said. "Almost. I was a kid the last time."

"I wondered if you'd ever grow up to be sensible."

"Sensible!" I snapped. "If I'm not sensible now—"

"You've proved to be exceptionally so," he broke in. "When I wrote to ask you to come, I had no idea what I was letting myself in for."

"And what did you discover?" I asked flippantly.

"You were certainly equal to the test."

"I should hope so!" I flared.

"Seriously, Amy, you took on a job I couldn't have done justice to. I don't blame you for wanting to leave us now."

"You asked me to do a job, and I did it. Now it's over, and I must go. It's as simple as that."

He stared silently at the west, watching the flame and tumult of a windy sunset spread across the sky. Then he turned back to me.

"I know, and believe me, I appreciate all you've done. I'm sure you'll be happy, back in your classroom."

I didn't answer, for a deep sadness seeped into my spirit when I thought of going away. I wouldn't be waking up in Meriweather Hall in the sweet bright mornings, knowing here was where I belonged.

Paul came toward me and placed his hands on my shoulders. "What's wrong, Amy? You look . . . sad."

"Oh, Paul, I haven't told Brandy I'm leaving because she's going to be so set on having me stay. But I've got to get on with my life, now that the problems here are solved." I turned my face away so he couldn't see the naked look of love I was sure shone in my eyes.

He stared at me for what seemed like a long time. Then he cupped my chin in his strong hands and tilted my face toward his.

"Brandy's stronger now that Corrie-Mom's recuperating. Snow White has helped, too. I think she'll handle your pullout better than you think. Especially if she knows you'll be back."

He grew quiet and dropped his hands.

I stared at my lap, embarrassed at the heavy silence between us. "But my job here is done. Why should I come back?" I said finally, awkwardly.

He took my hand and pulled me to my feet. I saw the dark, intense look on his face. He was the same gentle Paul I had known and loved so many years.

"Amy. . . ." His voice was husky. "Amy, I know it's too soon. The pain of losing Sue is still so sharp. We were both so young when we got married. Maybe what I felt for her was more pity than love—I'm not sure. But I know deep down I love you—have always loved you in a way I didn't realize until now. Please promise me you'll come back when you're ready. After school is out next spring, maybe? Will you come back? Marry me? I love you, Amy. You belong here, you know."

The wind gusted around the corner of the house with a shower of tattered leaves, and I shivered. But not from the cold.

"Yes, Paul. I'll be back," I whispered, trembling at his words. "I—I've loved you for so long. . . ."

He opened his arms then, and without a word I slipped into them, feeling suddenly safe and warm. His lips touched mine, then gently caressed my hair and throat. Suddenly I was kissing him back, knowing that his kind of love was real, his emotions trustworthy. Finally I laid my head against his shoulder, my pulse racing, as a wave of joy swept over me.

All the sadness, bewilderment, and trouble of the past six months had suddenly drained away. I knew I had to leave,

194

but there would be no intrigue, no mystery to greet me when I returned. Here at long last was God's love and harmony, the way it was meant to be. I knew that when I returned to Meriweather Hall it would be to a new beginning!

The Author

Esther Loewen Vogt was born in eastern Oklahoma to Mennonite parents who moved to a Kansas farm when she was eight. The middle daughter of five girls, Esther developed a deep hunger for reading during the Depression years. For this her mother called her "the Dreamer."

She dreamt of some day writing the kinds of stories she liked to read. But she pushed the desire aside because she considered herself a simple country girl. To her, writers were big people. Although her high school and college teachers urged her to develop her writing skills, she resisted. She graduated from Tabor College, Hillsboro, Kansas, in 1939, and taught in a country school for three years.

After her marriage to Curt Vogt in 1942, Esther settled down to be a good wife and mother to their three children. One day during her devotions as she read Matthew 25, the story of the talents gripped her in a profound way. It seemed as though God stepped from the page and shook his finger at her, telling her that if she didn't use her writing talents she would lose them.

In desperation she cried, "All right, Lord. I'll write—if you'll provide the opportunities!" That was the beginning of a long and rewarding writing career. Hundreds of short stories and sixteen published books later, she is still not through.

A widow since 1975, Esther still writes for a variety of denominations. Books have become her forte. She serves as part-time instructor for Christian Writers Institute, a correspondence course for budding writers based at Wheaton, Illinois. She also leads workshops at writing conferences.

Esther is an active member of the Hillsboro Mennonite Brethren Church, a member of Kansas Authors Club, and an honorary member of Delta Kappa Gamma in the Alpha Omega Chapter. She has won several awards: the David C. Cook Juvenile Book contest honorary award with *Turkey Red*, 1975; the Tabor College Alumni Merit Award, 1974; the Kansas Authors Club Literary Achievement Award, 1981; and the Outstanding Writer Award at the El Dorado Creative Writers Workshop, 1981.

Esther's three grandchildren look forward to the little stories Grandma writes just for them.